A Hopeless Discovery

A Hope Walker Mystery Book Three

Daniel Carson

Cover Design by Alchemy Book Covers
Formatting by Polgarus Studio
Editing by David Gatewood

∽ CHAPTER ONE ∽

I was halfway through one of Granny's double bacon double cheeseburgers when the call came in.

"Hope, it's Alex, and I've got something you need to see."

My name is Hope Walker, and I grew up in Hopeless, Idaho, the weirdest town in America. I was abandoned by my mother before I could walk. I was raised by my granny, who owns only one change of clothes—as well as a bar named the Library. And I left Hopeless when I was nineteen because a boy named Jimmy died.

But a series of recent unfortunate events brought me back home, and now instead of being a big-city, hotshot investigative reporter, I work as a small-town beat reporter for the *Hopeless News*. My boss, Earl Denton, pays me just enough so I feel terrible about myself, and I don't plan on working for him for very long.

But it's not all bad. It's been nice being with Granny again, and I love spending time with my old best friend, Katie. And then there's the new sheriff. Sure, he's a proud and frustrating sort of man, but he's also tall, dark, and looks great in a pair of jeans. And when he's not frustrating, he has a way of looking at me that makes me nervous. And that causes the memory of that boy named Jimmy to fade just a bit.

The sheriff's name is Alex Kramer. He was the one calling me, and his voice was all business.

"What is it?" I asked.

"Remember the deal we made?"

"The one where you were going to stop getting in my way and let me report the news of this town like the world-class investigator I am?"

"I knew this was a mistake."

You see, Sheriff Alex Kramer didn't like the fact that I had solved a double homicide my first week back in Hopeless. So when the Thorndales' family butler showed up dead, we made a deal. Or… maybe it was more like a bet. Whoever solved the case first was the winner. If Alex won, then I was to stay out of his way and leave the serious crime investigations to local law enforcement. But if I won, then he agreed to let me investigate whatever crimes occurred in our little town.

And I'll give you a little hint.

Alex didn't win.

"Relax, Sheriff, I'm only kidding. What's going on?"

"You know Lydell Clowder's place?"

"Mr. Clowder, the goat farmer? Sure."

"Then you need to get out here, and fast."

"What's wrong?"

"Hope, I can't believe I'm saying this—but our small town has got itself another dead body. And this time, I really need your help."

I took Highway 15 two miles out of town, past the spot where Jimmy died, past the old cabin I once upon a time wanted to live in, and turned left onto the tree side of Moose Mountain. On the other side of Moose Mountain, what locals affectionately called the slope side of the mountain, was Moose Lodge, where the skiing took place in the winter months. But on this side of the mountain, there was nothing but the thick trees of the Sawtooth and a dozen or so cabins that had been there so long they seemed almost as much a part of the natural landscape as the trees themselves.

When I was younger, Granny had spent a lot of time with me in these woods, and Mr. Clowder's goats were always fun for me to see, especially when I was very little. He let them roam through the forest, chewing up the overgrown plants. Granny said those goats were doing the rest of us a favor. Nature's lawnmowers, she called them. And it made the hiking easier for all of us.

But there would be no hiking today. I wound up the gravel mountain road to the Clowder place, where I found Alex standing in front of his sheriff's truck with his arms folded. As had become his custom, he wore a cowboy hat, a long coat, a flannel shirt, dark blue jeans, and cowboy boots. His gold star was placed prominently on his left lapel. He was tall, with wide shoulders and lean muscles, his jaw was strong, and he had a nice smile. Basically, he was good-looking in a slightly obnoxious way. But it was his eyes that got me. They were green and fierce, and when they looked at me, I had a tendency to get wobbly.

Thankfully, he was also a gigantic pain the rear. That was enough to make me safe around him.

As I stepped out of my car, he met me with a slight nod of his head, a dark expression on his face.

"Now, I don't know everything you've seen in your time as a big-city investigative reporter," he began, "but… well, I've never seen anything like this."

"It's that bad?"

"Afraid so."

Instead of leading me into the cabin, he steered me left toward a clearing. I could see Mr. Clowder's goats in the distance, poking their heads in and out of the trees as they scampered around, playing in the crisp October air. Alex strode straight to the middle of the clearing, where a black tarp was stretched out over something.

Of course, I knew what that something was. The body.

He grabbed one corner of the tarp and looked up at me. "You ready?"

Alex was right. I'd seen things in my time as a big-city reporter. And I'd already come face to face with murder in my brief time back in Hopeless. But I hoped to never get used to death. So I took a deep breath as I nodded. "Ready."

Alex pulled back the tarp.

I jumped back and let out a rather embarrassing shriek. I was *not* prepared for what was there. Not prepared at all.

There was indeed a dead body under that tarp…

… but it wasn't human.

It was gray and white, with a thick full beard… and four legs.

It was a goat.

～ CHAPTER TWO ～

"I hate you, Alex Kramer," I said as the not-so-good sheriff laughed uncontrollably.

"You should have seen your face, Hope! It was priceless."

"Priceless? You told me there was a dead body under there."

"There was. A dead goat body. I never said it was human."

"You told me to prepare myself—that you'd never seen anything like it."

"All true. It's my first dead goat. Seen plenty of dead animals. Lots of dead deer, a few cows, a horse once. But never a goat."

"You pulled me away from a perfectly greasy double bacon double cheeseburger just to pull a prank on me?"

Alex wagged a finger at me. "Now that's where you're wrong. I'd say, oh, maybe thirty percent of it was the prank. And for the record, that part was worth it. But the other seventy percent is official business. Like I said, a deal's a deal. I promise to not get in the way of you investigating crimes in this town. I'll even keep you in the loop. And this"—he gestured to the dead goat—"this is me keeping you in the loop."

"I don't think even Earl Denton cares much about a dead goat, Sheriff."

Alex smiled. Thankfully, he was being a butthead, so his gorgeous smile had no effect on me. He knelt down and pulled the tarp back even further. "Well," he said, "before you make any judgments about newsworthiness, wait until I tell you the whole story. This isn't just a dead goat."

I saw it immediately. Just under the goat's shoulder blade was a small hole surrounded by dried blood. An entry wound. I knelt down and saw that more blood had pooled beneath the body.

"The goat was shot?"

"No, Hope, not just shot. I just got done taking Mr. Clowder's full statement. And according to him? This goat… he was *murdered*."

"You can't be serious."

"I am. I am serious."

"Alex, what am I really doing here?"

"Like I said, we had a deal. And you were right, the sheriff's office is woefully understaffed. It would be foolish of me to refuse the help of an accomplished investigator such as yourself, especially considering she's only trying to do her job… not to mention her civic duty."

"I think we both know I wasn't talking about dead goats."

He stood up and shook his head. "I don't remember us

making any exceptions for goats. In fact, I don't recall saying anything about goats one way or the other." He scratched his chin thoughtfully. "Perhaps I should go back and look at the agreement, see if there was a goat section I've forgotten about…" Still looking thoughtful, he started off toward his truck.

"Now where are you going?"

"Like I said, we're woefully understaffed. Brooks Grady got his old station wagon stolen last night, so I need to go look for it."

"A stolen car? Why didn't you tell me about *that* one?"

Alex pointed toward the cabin. Old Mr. Clowder had come out onto the front steps and was looking our way.

"Because I told Mr. Clowder that I was bringing in the best homicide detective I knew to crack this case. He's waiting to talk to you." Alex got in his truck and started it up. He leaned out the window. "And Hope? The man's in serious grief, so I wouldn't keep him waiting too long. Well, off to deal with grand theft auto. Good luck with your murder investigation!"

He gave me an obnoxious grin and even had the nerve to wink at me. As he took off, I had just enough time to pick up a piece of gravel and clank it off the side of his truck.

I walked to my car. There was *no way* I was investigating a goat murder. But… I could feel Mr. Clowder staring at me. This crime, this… goat murder… it mattered to him.

Don't do it, Hope. Don't waste your time on this.

I spun around and looked at Mr. Clowder. He stood on his porch, his shoulders slumped, his face turned down. As far as I knew there had never been a Mrs. Clowder—just an old man and his goats. That old man was now grieving.

And he was expecting *me* to help him.

Stupid Alex Kramer.

As Mr. Clowder led me into his kitchen and poured me a cup of coffee, I looked around. The place was surprisingly cute—and clean—for a single man. No trash on the floor, no dirty underwear spread about, no empty soup cans lining the counter. Everything was in its proper place. The fireplace was crackling with a slow, steady fire, with a rocking chair set in front of it. A pair of reading glasses and a Bible rested on a small table.

And that's when my eyes went to the mantel over the fireplace. When I saw the pictures for the first time.

Mr. Clowder came up beside me and handed me a cup of coffee. "Yep, these are my kids."

On the mantel were dozens of small framed pictures… of goats. And off to one side were a couple hundred more small photos collected into a montage. Goats, goats, and more goats. Every last photo.

He pointed at the montage. "That's a memory board of past goats, but the ones on the mantel, these are my current goats." His lip began to quiver. "Well, that is… except for Percy." He pulled a picture from the mantel. It showed a white-and-gray goat with a hint of a smile. Mr. Clowder held the picture with pride, then pressed it to his chest. "My dearest Percy, cut down in the prime of his life."

I suddenly got the feeling that I was attending some sort of a goat wake. But as this was my first goat wake, I could only guess at the protocols. "I'm really sorry for your loss, Mr. Clowder."

"Not just my loss," he said. "*The world* lost one of the truly great goats today." He raised his cup of coffee, and I suddenly realized we were doing a toast. I raised my cup as well.

And then I realized Mr. Clowder was waiting for *me* to make a toast.

"Um... to Percy," I said hesitantly. "One of the best."

"To Percy!" Mr. Clowder threw back his coffee like it was a shot of tequila and wiped his hand across his face.

Before this got any weirder, I decided I had better start my investigation. "So, Mr. Clowder," I said. "Sheriff Kramer says you think Percy was murdered?"

"In cold blood. I assume you've seen the body?"

"Yeah, I saw that Percy was shot. But why do you think it was murder?"

"What do you mean?"

"Isn't it likely that some idiot hunter was shooting at turkey or deer and missed... and Percy was the unfortunate victim?"

Mr. Clowder frowned. "I've lived in this cabin for over forty years. Nothing like that has ever happened before."

"Well, it would be a freak thing," I replied, "so it wouldn't happen very often. Hunters do still hunt in these woods, don't they?"

"We've tried to scare them off... but yes, they do. But

I'm telling you, this was no hunter. This was deliberate."

"Okay, let's assume that's true. Who would want to kill Percy?"

He shrugged. "I don't know."

"Did he have any enemies?"

"Now you're making fun of me."

"No, I'm not. Just—look at it from my perspective, Mr. Clowder. To believe this is murder, I need a motive. What motive would anyone have to murder a goat?"

He shrugged. "I don't know. Why do people usually murder goats?"

"They don't. Nobody murders goats."

"Wolves murder goats."

"Well, yes, but they don't typically use guns."

"That's a fair point. Listen, I don't know what to tell you, Hope, but I know my goats. And Percy, he was one of the good ones."

I took a sip of coffee. "Not like those bad goats you're always hearing about."

Clowder nodded solemnly. "Exactly. Percy was the kind of goat a man could depend on. That's why I castrated him."

I spit out my coffee. "You what?"

"Percy was one of my wethers. I've got three of them. I keep Danny in with the bucks, but Percy and Leon stayed with the main herd."

"Mr. Clowder, I literally have no idea what you just said."

He looked at me curiously. "You don't know much about goats, do you?"

"I'm afraid they didn't feature prominently in my education."

"Then I need to fill in that gap. But first, a question. What do you call a goat with only one ear?"

"I don't know."

"Van Goat!" He laughed.

I was at a loss. "I—I'm sorry?"

"Van Goat! You know. Like the painter... with one ear?"

"Oh... right." I tried to smile. Apparently goat wakes also involved terrible jokes.

"Percy loved that joke. I'm gonna really miss that goat. Well, come on then. If you're gonna solve this goat crime, you're gonna need to know the difference between a buck and a wether. Heck, I might even let you milk some of the mamas."

"That's really not necessary," I said quickly.

He waved dismissively. "It ain't about necessary. It's learning."

"Well, I mean... I wouldn't want to mess anything up."

He nodded. "'Cause if you do, you know what we'd have to call it?"

I gave him a blank look. I had a bad feeling about this.

He smiled. "An udder disaster!"

"That's a good one, Mr. Clowder. I bet Percy loved it."

"You bet he did. Now follow me. We've got a murder to investigate."

~⟡ CHAPTER THREE ⟡~

Mr. Clowder led me outside, to a fenced-in area with a shelter at one side. Three goats wandered around, chewing on grass. As he leaned against the fence, all three goats looked up briefly before going back to their meal.

"The two larger ones are bucks. The smaller fella is a wether. A wether is a castrated male."

I tried not to look for his missing bits. Out of respect, I guess. "Why do you, uh… do that?"

"You see, people raise goats for their milk and their meat. I raise 'em for their milk, which I use to make cheese And to keep a good milk-producing herd, I need those mamas to keep having babies. And to keep having babies…"

"You need the bucks."

"Your granny taught you well. But I can't keep the bucks with the herd."

"Because they'd go girl crazy?"

"To put it kindly. But it's not just that. When the bucks are in rut, they stink something awful."

"Why's that? Pheromones?"

"No, not pheromones. They pee on themselves! Roll around in it. Cover themselves from head to toe. The girls love it. I call it goat cologne."

"Oh, well sure," I said. "Because who wouldn't love a bearded goat who smells like pee?"

Mr. Clowder slapped me on the back. "Now you're thinking like a goat. I like it."

I gestured toward the pen. "So I still don't understand why you have the uh… the wether. What's he there for?"

"Basically, to get picked on. If I left the bucks alone, they'd kill each other. Danny's here to give them someone else to pick on."

"Like a *scape goat*?" I said.

Mr. Clowder laughed. "Ha! That's great! Percy would've loved that."

Mr. Clowder then led me to the rest of the herd, which was wandering in and out of the trees on the edge of the pasture outside Clowder's cabin. There had to be at least fifty of them.

"I don't see any fence," I said.

"And you won't. I tried it when I was young, but it just didn't work for me. The more I let the goats wander about and choose their own food, the better the milk tasted. I figure a goat knows what it's supposed to eat better than I do."

"Do they always return home?"

He shook his head. "Not always. Like every parent, I get some runaways. Percy ran away when he was a youngster. I found him two days later in a rainstorm. Goats hate the rain.

When I found him, he was shivering and scared. I covered him with my coat, picked him up, and carried him back home. I think that day is what made us so close. And, you know—his sense of humor, of course."

"Of course," I agreed. "But you said you castrated him? That doesn't sound like something you do when you're... close."

Mr. Clowder shrugged. "He's a male, so he wasn't going to produce milk, and I sure wasn't gonna eat old Percy. But I figured he was so good-natured, he'd be a great wether. And he was. Everybody liked him." Mr. Clowder pointed toward a light-brown goat standing on a big rock. "That's Leon—he's my other wether. He's a good goat, too. But..." Mr. Clowder let out a sigh.

"But he's not Percy."

"Exactly."

Finally, we walked over to the tarp. It seemed like the rest of the herd was staying away on purpose. I sensed Mr. Clowder stiffen up as we got closer. He stopped a few feet short and rubbed his chin.

"I was inside drinking my mid-morning coffee when I heard the shot. At first I thought it was Van Brocklin shooting trap. He likes to do that occasionally. But then, I don't know why, I got a bad feeling. I came outside and saw the herd running away from the pasture. And right here, right on this spot, was Percy. By the time I reached him... he was already... gone." He choked up a bit, and I gave him a moment to collect himself.

Finally he took a deep breath and continued. "The good

news is, there's no blood trail, so I'm assuming he died pretty well instantly." Then he dropped to his knees and pointed to the forest. "And if you look at *how* he fell, I'm guessing the shot came from the woods. That would square with the sound. Van Brocklin's place is three or four hundred yards straight through the trees."

"But it also makes sense that a hunter would be shooting from the woods," I countered.

"Yeah, sure, but…" He shook his head.

"But what?"

"Well, I know you want to tell me it was a hunter, so let's say you're right. That means a hunter lines up a deer, misses, and *just happens* to hit an adult male goat so perfectly that he drops him dead on the spot?"

"Do you have a better explanation?" I asked.

Mr. Clowder's pocket buzzed. He pulled out a slick-looking iPhone and answered. "Clowder's Milk and Cheese, may I help you?" His head bobbed up and down for a moment. "Of course, just let me bring up your order." He covered the phone. "Excuse me, Hope, I need to take this call inside."

"Do you mind if I look around a bit more?"

"No, in fact I appreciate it. Listen, Hope, I know this probably isn't the kind of thing you normally do. Heck, it might seem silly, me fussing over an old goat like this. But Percy wasn't just a goat to me, and I'd really like to find out who did this."

"I understand, Mr. Clowder. I'll do what I can."

As Mr. Clowder returned to his cabin, I looked down at

the tarp that covered his beloved old friend, and I shook my head. Two months ago I was living in the vibrant city of Portland, working as an investigative reporter for the *Portland News Gazette*, putting the finishing touches on a year-long investigation of mob boss Tommy Medola. An investigation I thought would launch my career into the stratosphere. But that version of my life skidded off the rails, and now instead of a big-time investigation, I was standing in the middle of a pasture, trying to figure out how to make an old man feel better about a dead goat.

I pulled out my phone and called my best friend, Katie.

She answered on the first ring. "Yo."

"Did you know that Sheriff Kramer was going to trick me into a goat murder investigation?"

"No, but that sounds amazing, and I'm dying to hear all the scandalous details. But at the moment I'm trying to get everything ready to leave."

"To leave? Oh, crap, I forgot—you and Chris's *trip*."

"You said 'trip' in a really creepy way."

"Well, if you think about it, isn't the whole point of a weekend away from your kids kind of creepy?"

"Get your mind out of the gutter, Hope Walker. Not everything revolves around that."

"Does Chris know that?"

"Okay, that's a good point. Listen, the babysitter's supposed to be here any second, and I still have to finish setting up the electric fence for Dominic."

"Are you serious?"

"No, though it would be easier for the babysitter if I was.

Listen, Hope, if Dominic ties the babysitter up or superglues her to the kitchen chair, or anything else he might have learned from watching *Home Alone*, would you be willing to maybe come by and remind him that his mother's coming home in two days and that I know all the pressure points in the human body?"

"Katie, has it ever occurred to you that maybe Dominic is the way he is because of his dear mother?"

"I'll pretend you didn't say that, my now-*ex*-best-friend. I believe you have a goat murder to solve, and I've got to remember to pack my old lady underwear just in case."

"In case of what?"

"In case I need a break from our weekend away."

After I got off the phone with Katie, I took one more look at poor Percy. The bullet had gone into the side of his neck just above his front shoulder. He would have died almost instantly. If this was a hunting accident, Clowder was right: it was quite a miracle that the shot was so dead-on.

Assuming Percy didn't spin around before dropping dead, the shot would have come from the direction of the trees at the top of the hill. I started up that way to see if I could find any sign that a hunter might have been in the area.

But almost as soon as I crossed the tree line, the terrain changed, and I realized I was walking gently downhill. The slope descended another forty yards before leveling off, and then it remained flat for as far as I could see.

I turned and looked back the way I had come. Sure enough, it was a gradual but steady incline right to the edge of the trees. That marked the top of the ridgeline, and the pasture then descended on the other side.

I came to a sinking conclusion.

There was no way for a hunter to take a shot from within these woods and have it hit Percy. To do so it would have to travel uphill, over the ridgeline, and then magically turn in midair in order to travel downhill to the middle of Clowder's pasture. That meant if the shot really came from this direction, it had to have come from the top of the hill, right at the edge of the trees.

I jogged back up to the tree line and looked down toward Percy's body. I held out my hand as if I was shooting, and I tried to line myself up in the general area from which the shot would have been fired. It was hard to be precise, though, so I gave up and just started walking along the tree line, looking for clues. Perhaps a footprint, or a shell casing left behind by a careless fool.

Mostly what I found were hoofprints. But then I got lucky. When I spotted the clue, my heart leapt. It wasn't a shell casing. It was a folded half-sheet of paper.

I unfolded it to reveal two words, spelled out in cut-out magazine letters the way psychos did in the movies.

Bang Bang.

I spun around, my heart now pounding. I felt like someone was out there watching me.

I looked at the message again. Then back down the hill toward Percy. He may have been just an old goat, but Mr. Clowder was right. This was no accident.

I had no idea who did this, or why, but I knew one thing for certain.

This was cold-blooded murder.

~◦ CHAPTER FOUR ◦~

The creepy note wasn't my only clue. I also found a few footprints—human, not goat—nearby. They might have been Mr. Clowder's, but then again, they might not. I was just taking photos of them with my phone when it buzzed with a call from Katie.

"Aren't you supposed to be knee-deep in granny underwear by now?"

"At this rate, I'll be lucky if I take a shower this weekend. Hope, we've got a serious emergency."

"Dominic's already dropped a paint can on the babysitter's head?"

"For the record, I had Chris put all the paint cans under lock and key for exactly that reason. No, this is worse."

"He killed her?"

"Worse. She called and said she's sicker than she's ever been in her life. I told her to suck it up and take ibuprofen like the rest of us. She hung up on me. I've got no one to watch the kids, Hope!"

"Can you ask your mom?"

"She's busy, for real."

"And Chris's parents?"

"They're busy too, but not for real. My mother-in-law is scared of Dominic."

"Tell her to suck it up like the rest of us."

"Only in my dreams, Hope, only in my dreams."

"So what are you going to do?"

And then, something very frightening happened. My best friend was speechless.

Speechless Katie was never a good sign. Like when we were twelve years old and she was putting suntan lotion on my back at the pool, and I asked her if it was possible that green plant she'd picked up on the way was actually poison ivy. Or that time when we were in high school and I asked her if she'd remembered to put my car's parking brake on because it sometimes slipped out of park when it was on a hill. I'd never seen Katie run so fast in my life.

Speechless Katie always meant something bad. And this time, I had a feeling I knew what that something bad was.

"Uh-uh, Katie. No way."

"You owe me, Hope Walker."

"I can't watch your kids this weekend."

"Give me one good reason why not."

"I'm... really scared of Dominic too?"

"I know that's not true. In fact I do believe he's got a healthy fear of *you*."

"But I don't watch kids. You remember when I tried to take care of Simon Funkel's turtle that one time?"

"He was dead within twenty-four hours, I remember. I

wouldn't have thought it possible. But don't worry, Hope, my children are much more resilient than turtles. More like cockroaches, really. And like I said, you owe me."

"Please don't give me the you've-been-gone-twelve-years bit again."

"No, this is a specific subset of the gone-for-twelve-years bit. This is the specific part where you missed the birth of *all three* of my children. Since you weren't here for me then, you owe it to be here for me now."

"Birthing three children sounds better than watching your kids for an entire weekend."

"Spoken like a skinny single woman who's never given birth. You know what, Hope, I'm kind of glad the babysitter canceled. This is going to be good for you."

"*Good* for me? How?"

"In the same way that a life-threatening disease boosts your immune system for the rest of your life."

"That could be the advertising campaign to get people in Europe to have more children."

"Help me, Obi Wan Ke-Walker, you're my only Hope. You're Chris's only hope. Most important of all, you're granny underwear's only hope."

"I just threw up in my mouth a little bit."

"Welcome to parenthood. See you in five minutes."

I put the psycho note in my pocket, took a few more photos of the footprints, and made a mental note to follow back up with Mr. Clowder as soon as I could. I stopped in front of Percy's body on the way back to my car. What a sad way to go. Though… I wasn't actually sure how goats were supposed to die. Maybe jumping off some super-high cliff? Or having a heart attack from rolling around in too much pee? But I knew it wasn't being dropped from fifty yards by some psycho punk who leaves creepy "bang bang" notes.

Incredibly, I wanted justice for this old castrated goat.

But for now, justice would have to wait.

At least for the next few days, it was time to tackle the toughest job of all.

It was time to be a mom.

When I pulled up to Katie's house, Chris was putting luggage into the trunk of his car, and Katie was holding baby Celia in one hand and her keys in the other. As she handed me the keys, she smiled the large obnoxious smile of a woman who knew what the next few days of my life were going to look like.

"You'll be driving the minivan, Hope."

"I've never driven a minivan. Was sort of hoping to avoid that in my life."

"Nonsense. It's like a station wagon but not nearly as cool. Now remember, this ain't the 1980s. You have to use seat belts and car seats. Can't just duct tape the baby onto that little cushion between the two front seats."

"Any other weird rules?"

"Celia is a baby. Which means she doesn't poop on the toilet. She wears these things called diapers."

"I just threw up in my mouth again."

"Also, you have to feed the kids on a regular basis, and

they can't just drink beer and eat peanuts off the floor of Granny's bar."

"No wonder you're always so grouchy."

"Lastly, here's the number for Dominic's parole officer."

"You're kidding."

"It's the number for the pediatrician. If any of the kids swallow money or get a flower stuck up their nose, he's super good at getting them out."

"You're regular customers?"

"More like a subscription service. Like Medical Netflix for really crappy parents like us. There's a detailed schedule on the kitchen counter. If you can read, you'll be fine. If you can use a microwave, even better."

"A microwave?"

"I assume you don't cook."

"I was thinking takeout."

Katie smiled. "That would assume you had money or I was giving you some."

"Microwave it is."

Katie gave Celia a big kiss, then held her out to me. When I hesitated, Katie shook her head. "It's a baby, Hope. You hold her and feed her and just love her as best as you can."

"But what if she doesn't like me?"

"Then just leave her in a basket outside a convent. Until then, I'm afraid you're stuck with each other. Thanks for doing this."

"I'm pretty sure I haven't said yes."

"Not with your words, but with your terrible body

language. Seriously, I'll owe you one."

"You better not come back with another one of these."

"Kids? Hope, I'm not sure you follow the news, but our country isn't having enough kids to replace our population. Social Security is in jeopardy! Chris and I see it as our civic duty to help the country out."

She turned to her kids. "Now Dominic, do not burn down the house."

He stood straight and saluted. "Yes, Mama!"

"And Lucy, Aunt Hope's going to need a lot of help."

"Yes, Mama."

Almost the second Katie joined Chris in the car, he threw it in reverse and peeled out of there. Katie screamed with excitement and waved.

I adjusted Celia on my hip while I stared at Lucy and then Dominic. "So, what do you think we should do?" I asked.

"We could play Monopoly," Lucy suggested.

"But that takes hours."

Lucy smiled. "I know, isn't it great?"

"Dominic, what would you like to do?"

"We could put all the cushions in the front yard and then jump off the roof and see if it hurts."

"Monopoly it is!"

For the next two hours, I tried to keep most of my curse words under my breath. Holding a baby while one child tries to play Monopoly and the other child tries to blow up the Monopoly game is not my idea of a good time. I was actually relieved when Celia pooped, because it gave me a temporary timeout from Monopoly Hell.

But the game was never-ending. And when Dominic threw a clump of wet toilet paper in my hair just as I landed on Lucy's Park Place hotel, I decided I'd had more than enough.

I called Granny's bar.

"Library, Granny speaking. We've got a special on beer. We're selling it. And a special on turd balls. We don't tolerate 'em. Now what can I do for you?"

"Granny, it's me. I've got an emergency."

"Is this a real emergency or the kind of thing where I need to bail you out for something stupid you've done?"

"Somewhere in the middle?"

"I'm too old for this, Hope. And I was just about to call you. It seems you have a gentleman caller."

"What are you talking about?"

"I'm talking about the nice-looking young man that came into the bar two minutes ago looking for you."

"Alex?"

Granny cackled. "Heck no. This guy's name is Petterast. Oh, hang on now, he's telling me it's Pendergast. Mark Pendergast."

"I don't know him."

"Well darling, he knows you. Or your work. Says he's here to maybe offer you a job?"

"What are you talking about?"

"*I* don't know. That's just what the man said! If you want to talk to him, you better get down here."

"But that gets me to my emergency. I'm watching Katie's kids right now."

"Then come as soon as she's back."

"You don't understand. I'm watching her kids all weekend."

There was a moment of silence before Granny let out an obnoxious shriek of laughter. Then I heard her telling Bess that I was watching children, "*actual* children" all weekend. And *then* I heard her announce it to the bar. By the time she finally got back on the phone, my pride was officially at zero.

"You about done now?" I said.

"Oh, man, is that funny. My granddaughter watching children for a whole weekend."

"You know, once upon a time, I actually wanted to grow up and have children of my own."

"Yeah, and once upon a time I had a butt that didn't look like a clump of cottage cheese. Times change, my darling."

"You think if I came down to the Library to talk to this guy, you could maybe…"

"Do your job and watch her kids for you?" She sighed. "Well, I suppose since I've just taken my blood pressure medication… why not."

"Thanks, Granny, you're the best. Oh, and did he say anything about what kind of job?"

"As a matter of fact he did. Says he's with one of the big networks, and he's putting together a new investigative TV show. Seems like Mr. Pendergast wants you to be on TV."

~๑ CHAPTER FIVE ๑~

Just as I hung up the phone, Celia threw a handful of yogurt in my face. I screamed, which scared her, meaning I had to spend the next five minutes calming her down. Then I tried to set her down so I could jump in the shower and wash said yogurt off my face. But when I set her down she started to cry again.

"Lucy, how am I supposed to take a shower if every time I set her down she starts to cry?"

Lucy raised a finger. "You could just take her into the shower with you."

"Is that what your mama does?"

Lucy's eyes widened. "You want to do what mama does? Just a second." She skittered away, then reappeared with a package of wet wipes and a stick of deodorant.

"What's this?"

Lucy smiled. "This is how Mama takes a shower most days."

A good-looking TV guy was waiting down at the Library to speak with me about a job, and I had a clump of yogurt splattered all over my face and hair. I needed more than just a few wet wipes.

I set Celia down again, and immediately she started to scream. "Is there any way you could hold Celia for me?" I asked Lucy.

She shrugged. "When she gets this way, Mama's the only one who can keep her happy. But you're doing a pretty good job."

I took a deep breath, then carried Celia, the wet wipes, the deodorant, and the very little dignity I had left to the bathroom. I spent the next five minutes pretending baby wipes were a shower nozzle and deodorant was lavender soap. When I was done, I looked only slightly less crappy than before.

I spent the next fifteen minutes getting the kids ready, then I buckled them into their car seats and went to start the car, only to realize I didn't have the keys.

"Son of a—" I stopped myself when I saw Lucy and Dominic looking at me in the rearview mirror.

"Son of a what?" asked Dominic.

"Um… planter. George Washington was the son of a planter. That's your famous fact for the day, kids."

"Oh," said Dominic with a giggle, "I thought you were going to say the really bad word that Mama always says."

I ran back into the house and rummaged through the chaos of the kitchen until I found the car keys that Katie had given me. Then I ran back to the van, and finally we were off. Five minutes later, I was parked in front of the Library and hunched over the back seat unbuckling the kids from their car seats.

"Why are you breathing so funny?" Lucy asked.

I wasn't breathing funny so much as I was breathing heavily. Holy bananas, getting kids in and out of the car was exhausting. By the time I grabbed baby Celia, my pits were fully wet, and I was very glad I had applied a thin veneer of deodorant to every inch of my body.

I stubbed my toe against the curb, just managed to get my balance before launching Celia into Main Street, and hustled the kids to the door of the Library. By this point, I was certain I was going to pass out.

Note to self: stop getting on Katie's case for not working out. And never, ever admit to her how hard this is.

We walked into the Library just in time to see Granny lighting her whiskey breath on fire. This was one of her favorite bar tricks. She'd learned it when she was only eight years old and she got lost at the circus. According to the story, one I'd heard many times, Granny got found by some carnies and convinced them to let her play poker with them. That was a mistake… for the carnies. Within an hour, she'd taken all of their money. And since she was only eight, she didn't care so much about the money, so she said she'd give the money back if she could learn a genuine circus trick. The bearded lady asked if Granny liked the taste of whiskey… and the rest was history. Granny became the greatest fire-breather in all of central Idaho.

Dominic squealed. "Can Granny teach *me* how to breathe fire?"

Granny bent down and glared at him. "Only on one condition."

"Anything."

"How are you at Texas Hold 'Em?"

I handed Celia to Granny, and she nodded me toward a man at the far end of the bar. "That's Pendergast."

"And he's from Hollywood?"

"New York. Not a bad-looking feller." She looked me up and down, and frowned. "Though I've seen *you* have better days." She leaned forward and sniffed. "And why do you smell like a bed of flowers?"

"Do I really look that bad?"

"You'd be the best-looking gal in the entire emergency room."

"Seriously?"

"I'll have Bess turn the lights down a bit." She slapped me in the shoulder with her free hand. "Good luck, honey. Time to go teach these kids about poker."

I wanted to check a mirror and make a last-minute adjustment, but Mr. Pendergast was already looking right at me. So instead I remembered what Granny told me when I was younger and worried that my boobs weren't coming in. She stared at my chest like she was mining for buried treasure, then finally looked up as if she had my diagnosis. "Well, Hope, you may never have boobs, but you know what you *can* have? Confidence. No matter what situation you're in, stand up straight, throw your shoulders back, smile like an idiot, and own the room."

And that's what I did. I stood up a little taller, threw my shoulders back, and aimed for Mr. Pendergast. I was, after all, the best investigative reporter in the world. My talents were being wasted in Hopeless, and I was the right woman for whatever job Mr. Pendergast had. I hadn't thought of doing TV before, but why not? CNN and Fox News had hired two entire networks full of morons; surely there was at least one role for a woman with a gift for finding bodies and solving murders.

When Mr. Pendergast saw me coming, he smiled and nodded, then tapped something on his phone and slipped it into his pocket. Granny was right: he was handsome. He wasn't especially tall, but not short either. Probably five ten, five eleven, with the fit physique of a soccer player. His beard was dark and closely trimmed, and circular specs framed intense eyes. As I neared he straightened himself up and stuck out his own chest. Maybe Mr. Pendergast had small boobs too.

"Hope Walker, I presume?"

"At your service." I stuck out my hand out, and he took it. I squeezed, and he held on for an extra second before letting it go.

"Can I buy you a—"

"Bess!" I hollered. "One Stella!"

He chuckled. "Forgot. Your grandmother runs this place."

"And I live upstairs."

"And how is life above a bar?"

"Not quite as glamorous as you'd imagine."

He laughed.

"So, my granny says you wanted to see me, Mr. Pendergast?"

"Call me Mark."

"Then call me Hope."

He paused, like he was studying me. In another life, I'd think he was checking me out. But this man was here on business.

He took another drink. "I'm very interested in your work, Hope."

"Which work?"

"I've read all of your stuff from the *Portland Gazette*. Hard-hitting, insightful—you have a gift for picking up on a really compelling narrative through line, plus you've got just enough personality."

"You do realize I don't work for the *Gazette* any more, right?"

"Which makes you suddenly available, doesn't it?" He smiled. "Mind telling me the story behind your departure?"

Bess handed me the Stella, and I took a long sip.

"Not much to tell. I was working on the story of my life, and the paper was too chicken to run it."

"I figured as much. I didn't show up here in Hopeless without doing a little background first, Hope. And I've talked to enough people to figure out that someone is blackballing you."

"But you didn't know why."

He rubbed his dark black beard. Yep, Mark Pendergast was a good-looking guy. And business or no business, I didn't hate having drinks with him. "Still don't know why," he said. "Care to elaborate?"

"My guess is Tommy Medola doesn't want me to tell his story."

Mark's eyes narrowed. "Medola? As in the Medola crime family?"

"The one and only."

He looked away and scratched at his chin like a piece of his puzzle had just fit together. "So Medola gets wind of your story, pressures the newspaper to shut it down… and pressures every other newspaper to make you persona non grata."

"And *that's* why I'm back in my hometown, living above my granny's bar."

Mark took another sip of his drink, then pulled out his phone and looked at some messages like I wasn't even there. Finally he put it away and turned back to me.

He leaned in. "Listen, Hope, I'm sorry for your troubles… I really am. But maybe fate is playing a part in this drama. Maybe fate wants you to tell your story in a different medium."

"Television?"

He nodded. "I'm putting together a new newsmagazine for the networks."

"Like *60 Minutes*?"

He scoffed. "*60 Minutes* is a prescription for insomnia. I think half of those anchors are legally dead. No, what we're doing is the *next generation* of magazine shows. Younger. Hipper. Edgier. And, if I may say…" He smiled. "Better-looking."

Of course I knew he wanted to flatter me. But genuine or not, it felt good.

I took another drink. "That Ed Bradley's still quite the looker."

"I'll tell him you said that."

I grabbed his forearm. "You know Ed Bradley?"

"Hope, New York City is the largest small town in the world. And the news business is especially small. I know everyone. Well, everyone who's important."

"Then why are you in the weirdest town in America talking to me?"

He hesitated just a beat. "I'd heard about you—read your work. And I was in Sun Valley for business and thought, what the heck. Maybe we could chat. So I did my homework, and here I am."

"I'll be honest, Mark Pendergast—you've piqued my interest."

He tilted his head and smiled. It was a nice smile, with good teeth. And I imagined somewhere under that beard was a dimple. "Very good," he said.

"What do you need to know?"

"Is that Medola story ready for prime time?"

"Now?"

"Yes, now."

"I'm not sure."

"I thought you said your editor was chicken."

"He was. So was the owner. But Medola's lawyers said there are holes in my story. Said I flat-out lied."

"That's not good."

"What would you expect a criminal to say? But regardless, I need to see that list of what they said I lied about… and then… well, prove them wrong."

"Okay." He nodded, as if thinking this over. "Until

then… you got any other stories you're working on?"

"I've solved a few murders since I've been in town."

"One of the reasons I'm here. Terrific stories by the way. Just one problem: they're the property of the *Hopeless News*. Got anything else brewing?"

"Right now?"

"Yes. Right now. Ongoing."

"I just happened to catch a case this morning."

He opened his hands like we were in business. "Great. What is it?"

"Another murder."

"Remind me not to stay in Hopeless very long. Who's the victim?"

"His name's Percy. Gunshot victim."

"Anything particularly interesting about this one?"

"Percy was castrated."

Mark's eyes widened. "Are you kidding me?"

"Nope. There's one more thing."

Now he was hooked. "What's that?"

"Percy's a goat."

Mark was clearly very confused. "He's a castrated man who thinks he's a goat?"

"No, he's a castrated goat who thinks he's a goat. Correctly, as it turns out. And his owner thinks he was deliberately gunned down in the prime of his life."

Mark looked down and laughed. "I'm guessing my Manhattan audience won't be particularly interested in a story about a dead goat from Idaho."

"A *castrated* dead goat from Idaho. Don't forget the

castrated part. That's the sizzle viewers are looking for."

"Listen, Hope… I'll be honest with you. You're one of several people I'm looking at for this show. And all the others are talented. Very talented. Every one of them's got solid news chops. But I've gotten to where I am by trusting my intuition. And right now…" He reached out and touched my hand. "I like what I see."

He stood and put a twenty-dollar tip down on the bar. Then he handed me a card. "I'm headed to Sun Valley for business in the morning. There's a media conference all week. But I'll come back through town next weekend. Was hoping you and I could get dinner?"

"Dinner?"

"So we can… get to know each other better. Would you like that?"

Mr. Mark Pendergast, of soccer physique and dark beard, appeared to be a man who was accustomed to getting what he wanted. And that made him even more attractive. But it also scared me. I wasn't sure if I wanted to get to know him better.

But I *did* want to hear more about his job. So when he held out his hand, I took it.

"Yes," I said. "I think I'd like that just fine."

∼⌐ CHAPTER SIX ⌐∼

My excitement about the potential TV job vanished the moment Granny handed me a bucket and a mop, pointed to Celia, and said "Cleanup on aisle two!"

I wasn't sure what exactly I was cleaning off of Celia, but it wasn't natural. It seemed like something out of a Stephen King novel.

The nightmare continued at home. Celia, apparently, didn't believe in being put down—ever. I was able to calm her down, but every time I laid her in her crib, she would instantly wake up and begin to cry. And so it was back to my arms, where I rocked her and swayed back and forth. This dance continued for an hour before she finally gave up and went to sleep.

It was at that point that I went to check on Lucy and Dominic, hoping beyond hope that they were already nestled in their beds.

They were not.

Lucy had piled a large stack of books in the middle of the bedroom floor, and Dominic had popped a bag of microwave popcorn. They both pointed at the books.

"Read!" they yelled in unison.

It took four princess books, three Spider-Man books, and two nursery rhyme books for Dominic to fall asleep, his face pressed against the greasy popcorn bag. I cleaned his face off, carried him to bed, and tucked Lucy in as well.

I was just about to leave when I heard her sweet little voice say, "You forgot to pray."

And so we prayed. And when we finished our prayers, and I dragged myself to my own bed, I felt like I had just run some sort of domestic Iron Man contest. I had a brand-new appreciation for Katie and all she went through on a daily basis. And despite my excitement about Mr. Mark Pendergast and his new TV show, I had no trouble whatsoever falling asleep once my head hit that pillow.

Unfortunately, that didn't last very long.

The baby woke up in the middle of the night. I thought it was the fire alarm at first, but once I got my bearings and realized what was happening, I ran in there to get her before she woke up the other kids.

Unfortunately, when I picked her up she continued to cry. It was then that I smelled the *reason* why she was crying. Boy, did I smell it.

And trust me, it looked exactly like it smelled. Call it Creature from the Black Lagoon 2.0. Seriously, how does something like that come out of a baby that cute? I changed her, rocked her back to sleep—in only thirty minutes this time—then went into the bathroom to clean up.

What I saw in the mirror was not a pretty sight.

It was then I realized, now was my chance to take an actual shower. With water. Two o'clock in the morning? Why not.

Once I was clean, I found that I was wide awake, so I plopped on the couch and flipped through some infomercials. I estimated if I could just come up with $479, I could have tight abs, clean teeth, perfect skin, I could fry a turkey in my bathtub, and I could remove all the hair from my legs for a year.

At some point I must have fallen asleep, because when a finger started poking me in the shoulder, I had no idea what was going on.

I opened my eyes to find Dominic mere inches from my face. He was shaking.

"I had a bad dream," he sniffled.

Dominic was the kid who terrorized people with Nerf guns, let the air out of your tires, and watched horror flicks with his Mama. I wouldn't have thought it was possible for him to have a bad dream.

"What was it about?" I asked.

He sniffled. "Santa Claus. He... he brought me a Barbie doll!"

So *that* was the kind of thing that gave Dominic Rodgers nightmares. You live, you learn.

Without even asking, he climbed into my arms and nestled his head against my shoulder.

"Mama holds me when I have a bad dream."

"She does?"

He nodded. "And she usually whispers more of those bad words, so if you want to do that, it's okay with me."

I didn't whisper the bad words, but did hold Dominic. Within minutes, he was snoring away. I thought about this crazy chaotic life that Katie lived, that I hardly knew anything about. And I realized how much I had missed by being gone all these years.

I finally fell asleep again myself, only to wake up what seemed like just a few minutes later. But clearly I'd been out much longer than that. The sun was pouring through the windows, and Lucy and Dominic were jumping up and down on the ottoman in front of me.

"Bubba's! Bubba's! Bubba's!" they yelled in unison.

"I hope to God I'm having a nightmare and I actually have eight more hours to sleep."

Lucy smiled. "Silly Aunt Hope, today's the day we go to Bubba's Pumpkin Patch."

"Isn't today the day you all watch cartoons and order takeout and let me sleep like a normal human being?"

"It's right there on the schedule Mama left you. Today's the special day at the pumpkin patch where kids get their faces painted for free. *I'm* going to be a fairy princess!"

Dominic smiled. "And *I'm* going to be a flesh-eating zombie vampire!"

"Dominic, seriously—even *you* must be aware that you have problems, right?"

Unfortunately, Katie's schedule confirmed it: today, I was supposed to take the children to Bubba's Pumpkin Patch. It was something of a fall tradition around here for parents to take their children to Bubba's.

Key word: parents.

"Interesting that your mom picked today as the day for your visit to the pumpkin patch."

Lucy smiled. "Today's a special day. Every kid gets in for half price."

"So there will be lots of kids there today?"

Lucy smiled even wider. "Millions."

I'd rather not talk about the next hour of my life. About what exactly it took to get those kids and myself ready for a day at the pumpkin patch. I'm sure one day I'll talk about it in some sort of deep immersive therapy session... but until then, I'd rather act like it never happened. All I know for sure is that we arrived at the pumpkin patch at nine thirty along with, apparently, every other family in central Idaho.

I was grumpy and tired, carrying a backpack full of sandwiches and water bottles and fish crackers and diapers, and pushing Celia in a stroller, but Dominic and Lucy approached Bubba's with wide eyes as if they were having some sort of mystical experience. And I'll admit, even though I'd barely slept, most of my body hurt, and my hands smelled like a strange combination of poop and wet wipe, being back at Bubba's started having an effect on me as well. I'd always thought of it as a pretty magical place when I was little, and from the looks of it, Bubba's had really grown up. I remembered a modest pumpkin patch with hayrack rides, a little haunted house, and a mechanical dragon that ate pumpkins. The place we were entering looked more like Disney World.

Lucy had gotten a Bubba's map—that was new, too— and had it spread across Dominic's back in order to devise a plan of action for the day. "I say we get our faces painted first, then we'll do the bounce house explosion, then we can visit Wanda's World, and then—"

"Did you say Wanda's World?" I interrupted.

She nodded.

"I remember Wanda's World. That's with the mechanical dragon that eats the pumpkins, right?" That really had me feeling nostalgic. I remembered Granny laughing while the mechanical dragon chomped down on the pumpkins, spraying bits of pumpkin juice all over the people in the first two rows. "Would you mind if we visited Wanda's World first?"

Lucy smiled. "Sure, Aunt Hope!"

As we walked past Pumpkin Alley, Dominic pointed out thirty-seven different pumpkins that he wanted to take home. Lucy, the wise older sister, reminded him that it was more fun to pick the pumpkins straight from the patch.

We then walked down Apple Donut Lane, a boulevard for the best kinds of festival food you could possibly imagine. I'd like to say I had enough willpower to ignore the spectacular smells... but I would be lying. Instead I walked straight to the centerpiece of Apple Donut Lane: Lucinda's Famous Apple Donuts. I bought three donuts, and the kids and I devoured them.

So. Good. I made a mental note never to share those donuts with anyone ever again.

And then we arrived at Wanda's World. Its large metal sign, the same one I remembered from my youth, announced Wanda's World with a vintage look that gave off a serious "junkyard cool" vibe.

"It's just like I remember!" I said.

Wanda's World was named after some old lady named Wanda who built these fantastic metal beasts from scrap metal and then made them move like robots. The pumpkin-eating dragon was the first of these robots, and the most famous, but over the years she'd continued to add a variety of other beasts. Bears, unicorns, a pretty good Frankenstein, and more. All made of beaten-up junk, all moving in the herky-jerky manner of someone "doing the robot." It was like entering a mechanical zoo of misfit beasts.

The dragon ate pumpkins every hour on the half hour, and we had just missed a feeding—well worth it for those donuts. There was no way the kids would stand around that long, so we decided to go down the dirt road to the haunted house—though I first made the kids promise we'd come back.

Celia and I sat outside the haunted house while Lucy and Dominic went in alone. When they came back out five minutes later, Lucy was visibly shaken, while Dominic was smiling ear to ear.

"A guy started chasing us with a chainsaw!" Dominic screeched. "It was *awesome!*"

I truly think it was the highlight of the young boy's life.

The face-painting booth was next. We waited in line for fifteen minutes, which gave Dominic time to think of the most disturbing face paint possible. In the end, he went with half Freddy Krueger and half flesh-eating zombie vampire. Celia cried as soon as she saw him. Lucy stuck to her original plan of becoming a unicorn princess.

We went to the petting barn, where the baby goats were a huge hit. We watched a man put a giant pumpkin in a slingshot and launch it two hundred yards, where it crashed through the windshield of beat-up old pickup truck. We attended a chicken race where the chickens were dressed like jockeys. We ate caramel corn and shared a giant turkey leg. And it's possible I ate another warm apple donut. Or three. The only thing I refused to do was the corn maze, as I was still traumatized by a rather terrifying experience I had there when I was young. Corn maze, heavy fog, scared kid—you get the picture.

We did lots of other things that didn't exist at Bubba's when I was a kid. I even changed Celia right in the middle of a dirt road while a snooty woman glared at me like I was in over my head. I definitely never did that when I was a kid.

But by mid-afternoon, Celia was getting cranky, and so was I. It was time to get her home and hopefully down for a much-needed nap. I wouldn't mind a nap myself.

"But we can't leave without getting a pumpkin," protested the half-serial-killer, half-walking-dead five-year-old in my charge. And so the cranky baby and her cranky Aunt Hope followed Lucy and Dominic to the pumpkin patch.

That's right, there was still an actual pumpkin patch in the midst of this theme park.

Bubba himself organized the hordes of children into what looked like the starting line for the Boston Marathon. And then he raised a megaphone to his lips, and his might voice boomed. "One, two, *three!*"

The children descended into the pumpkin patch like a pack of wolves, and Bubba chuckled—just like he'd done when I was a kid.

And that's when my phone buzzed in my pocket, and I remembered that I had a completely other life that didn't involve wet wipes and cranky children and strollers and Bubba's. I looked at the number and felt myself smile in spite of myself.

"Hello, Sheriff."

"Hi, Hope, it's Alex."

"I know it's Alex. There's this thing called caller ID. Been around for thirty years or so. Common to one hundred percent of cell phones."

"You're really delightful to talk to, you know that?"

"Says the man who bamboozled me into a goat murder case."

Alex laughed. "In fact I was just calling to see if you'd made any headway on your investigation."

"I bet you think you're pretty funny."

"I do, as a matter of fact."

I imagined him smiling as he said it. Chiseled jaw. Brilliant green eyes. Smile that made me go weak. *Easy, Hope.*

"Well, Sheriff…" I started.

"It's Alex," he interrupted.

"I know it's Alex, but when you're being a butthead, I call you Sheriff. So, Sheriff, I have no leads at this time. Not that I've had any time."

"I heard. Apparently Hope Walker has opened a day care."

"Katie told you?"

"She could hardly stop laughing. I think this brings her a great amount of joy."

"And what, you're just calling to rub it in?"

"Pretty much. I also heard there's a fancy-pants Hollywood guy in town to see you."

"How'd you know about that?"

"I'm the butthead sheriff—it's my job to know about stuff like that."

"It's your job to know about the men in my life?"

Alex paused. "I didn't know he was a man in your life. The way I heard it, he wanted to talk to you about a job."

"And yet somehow he asked me out on a date in the process."

There was a much longer pause.

"Alex, you still there?"

"He asked you out on a date?"

That tone. I knew that tone. That tone wasn't curiosity. That tone was something else.

Lucy emerged from the pumpkin patch with a giant pumpkin, Dominic the horrible right behind her. "Sorry Alex, gotta run. With kids and goat murders and dates with hot Hollywood guys, I've got a busy life."

I ended the call before Alex could say anything else, and yes, I felt quite satisfied with myself. Did I lie about having a date with the Hollywood bigshot? A little. But did Alex lie to me when he told me he had a murder for me to investigate? A little. Now we were a little even. Maybe better than even. Because now I had secret information.

I was making Alex Kramer jealous.

Lucy was holding her perfect pumpkin like a proud mom holding a newborn baby. She had chosen well.

And then Dominic stepped from behind her to show me his.

Unfortunately, it was not a pumpkin. Which was probably why he was so happy. It was a bone. Make that two bones. Human arm bones, by the look of it.

Of course, this *was* Bubba's Pumpkin Patch. They probably kept spooky artifacts like this scattered about to amuse little psychopaths like Dominic. But I had a bad feeling about this.

I grabbed Dominic and ushered him quickly over to Bubba. Bubba gave me the peculiar look that I'd become used to over the last few weeks. Of people recognizing you but not sure *why* they recognize you.

"Hi, Bubba. Is there any chance you hide fake skeleton parts in the pumpkin patch just for kicks and giggles?"

"What are you talking about?"

Dominic excitedly hoisted his arm bones into the air for Bubba to see.

"I'm talking about this," I said. "This adorable little child just found these remarkably human-looking bones in your pumpkin patch."

The horrified look on Bubba's face was all the answer I needed.

I called Alex back.

"Hope, are you really going on a date with that—"

I cut him off. "Alex, you know how dead bodies keep

popping up around me?"

There was a long pause on the other end of the line. "Hope, you're not serious."

"No, but I *am* humerus. And… maybe radius or ulna? It's hard to be sure."

"What are you talking about?"

"Just come down to Bubba's, make your way down Apple Donut Lane past the haunted house, and you'll find me at the pumpkin patch, where a pint-sized Freddy Krueger has just discovered what I'm pretty sure are the partial remains of a human body."

～ CHAPTER SEVEN ～

Within twenty minutes, Sheriff Kramer had set up yellow police tape around the area of the pumpkin patch where Dominic had found the bones. Then the sheriff and his shovel got to work.

Bubba had moved his customers way back, but he and his wife, Mary, held each other and looked on in stunned silence. Surrounding them were other employees, all looking on intently as this body was uncovered in their midst. An older man with blue overalls and a green John Deere cap stood right behind Bubba and Mary, and beside him was a younger guy, maybe late twenties, black spiky hair, slightly nerdy. Most important was a sturdy young woman with brown skin who must have been from Apple Donut Lane, because when she saw me with the kids, she disappeared for a bit and came back with a wide smile and a paper bag of donuts for us. The donuts were a big hit, and Lucy and Dominic and even Celia munched down on that warm chewy goodness while Dominic kept boasting with pride about the greatest day of his young life. "Can you believe it,

Lucy? I really found a dead person's arm!"

After an hour of careful digging, Alex had uncovered the rest of the skeleton. He stepped away from the body and made a phone call, then he motioned for Bubba and Mary to come over. I took that as my cue to join them.

"So I just called the forensic anthropologist with the FBI in Salt Lake City. They're going to try and identify the body for us. But if either of you have any idea who this might be, that would really help me out."

Bubba and Mary looked at each other somberly, then turned toward the sheriff and said, "Wanda."

"Wanda from Wanda's World?" I asked.

Bubba nodded.

"I take it this Wanda worked for you?" Alex asked.

Bubba got choked up, so Mary answered. "Her name is… or was… Wanda Wegman. She'd been with us for… well, forever. From almost the beginning."

"And what makes you think this body is hers?" I asked.

Bubba wiped his cheeks. "She ran off three years ago, at the end of the season. We haven't heard from her since."

"Did you report this to Sheriff Kline?" asked Alex.

Bubba shook his head. "There wasn't a reason to. You see, Wanda… she was brilliant, but she was also stubborn and willful and a bit of a pain. We didn't always see eye to eye."

"You'd argue?" said Alex.

"Sure. But not just me. Wanda argued with everyone."

"It was just her nature," added Mary. "But we loved her. Deep down, everyone loved her."

"Then why didn't you report her missing?" I asked.

Bubba shrugged. "Because it wasn't the first time she'd left. Over the last twenty years, I bet she left, oh, how many times would you say, Mary?"

"Three or four at least."

Bubba nodded. "One time it was a few weeks. One time she went on a cruise and came back in the spring. Heck, one time she didn't show up until a few days before the season began."

"And this time?" asked Alex.

Bubba shrugged. "When she didn't show up for the next season... I figured she'd gone and left for good. That she'd finally had enough." He sniffled. "I had hoped to see her again one day."

Mary sighed. "But not like this. Not... murdered."

Sheriff Kramer held up his palms. "Let's just take a breath on that. All we've got right now is bones. I know you think this must be Wanda, but until we've got a positive ID, we won't know. And we don't know if this was a homicide."

Mary looked up with a strange look. "What else could it be?"

Alex shrugged. "Sometimes people just die."

"And bury themselves?" Bubba asked.

Before Alex could answer, Mary said, "How long will it take before there's a positive ID?"

"If they can match dental records, not too long. Otherwise, weeks."

"Can... we stay open?" she asked.

Bubba shot her a look, and Mary shrugged.

The sheriff looked around as if considering, then finally nodded. "You'll have to have this section of the patch closed, but otherwise, I don't see why not."

"In the meantime, what can we do to help?" Bubba asked.

Alex handed Mary a card. "Can you email a list of all your employees along with their contact info?"

"We have a lot of employees. Many weren't here when Wanda was around."

"How about your full-time employees?"

"Other than me and Bubba, there was Wanda, and…" Mary looked over to where the other employees were clustered. She pointed at the kind donut lady. "That's Lucinda Meadows, the Donut Queen. Next to her is Kip Granger, the farmer, and next to him is Johnny Driscoll, who handles our computers."

"Well, get me their contact info, along with the info for any part-time employees who might have known Wanda when she was here."

"Will do," said Bubba. "Anything else?"

Alex took his hat off and ran his hand through his hair. "I'll let you know."

As Bubba and Mary walked back to their employees, Alex turned to me. "I'm starting to get nervous around you."

I smiled. "I make you nervous, Alex Kramer?"

"Not like that."

"Oh, I *don't* make you nervous?"

"Hope, can you be serious for a second? How exactly do you keep stumbling upon dead bodies all the time?"

"It's a gift. I was voted Most Likely to Stumble Upon Dead Bodies in my senior yearbook."

"You really think this is funny, don't you?"

"For the record, I don't think anything having to do with finding dead bodies is funny."

"There's something we can agree on. Now, I have an important job for you to do."

"You're taking me off the goat murder case and making me your lead investigator on this one."

"No. I've got a phone number. And you need to call it."

Alex turned his phone around, and I looked at the number on the screen.

"Hey, I know that number. That's…" I started to panic. "That's Katie's number!"

"I know, Hope. And you have to tell her."

"Tell her that her son found a dead body while I was watching him?"

He gave me a sympathetic look. "Something like that."

"Not gonna happen. This is Katie's weekend to get away and have a little romance, and then when she's tired of romance, to wear nothing but granny underwear and watch Lifetime movies and drink margaritas. It is *not* her weekend to worry about things like taking care of kids."

"And finding dead bodies."

"Exactly!"

"So you're going to call her?"

"Not in a million years."

"Hope!"

I pointed to the kids. Dominic had a donut hanging out

of his mouth and was making disgusting snorting noises, and Lucy was giggling like crazy. "Do they look traumatized to you?"

Alex shook his head at me in disappointment, but before he could chastise me further, his phone rang, and he stepped away.

And I took a deep breath… and called Katie.

She picked up on the second ring. "Hope Walker, my new old friend, how is life with three children?"

"You're never going to believe what happened today."

"What?"

"Dominic… he…"

"He what, Hope? Dominic what?"

She sounded upset. Of *course* she sounded upset. I'd just interrupted her time away.

I just couldn't tell her the truth.

"He, um… couldn't decide whether he wanted to be Freddy Krueger or a flesh-eating zombie… so he's both."

"*That's* what you called to tell me?"

"It was really dramatic—not many people could pull it off. But he, um… he really did."

Katie giggled. "That's my adorable little psychopath. Other than that, everything going okay?"

"Oh, yeah, big-time okay. Uneventful. And you?"

"I have not moved from this bed in six hours."

"That's terrible. You should get out and do something fun."

"Are you kidding me? It's been the greatest six hours of my life. I don't think I'm ever coming back."

"Katie, you have to come back."

"Not really, Chris and I changed our will, and you now get sole custody of the children. So if a meteor hits our hotel room tonight, you're in charge."

"That's not a funny thing to joke about," I said.

"When you're lying in bed for six hours not taking care of your three children, it sort of is."

~◦ CHAPTER EIGHT ◦~

Celia fell asleep within five minutes of leaving Bubba's. And Lucy informed me that the only way to *keep* her asleep was to drive her around.

"For how long?" I asked.

"For as long as you want her asleep."

I gave Lucy and Dominic suckers out of the bag Katie had labeled "Emergency Suckers," told them to look for flying squirrels and unicorns, and put on some good music. And then I just drove.

Once upon a time, before jobs and responsibilities and heartache… *just driving* was my favorite pastime.

When I was little, and the days were turning from cold to tolerable, Granny would roll the windows down and just drive through the forest and the mountains with no particular destination in mind. When I was sixteen, Katie and I would turn the music way up, scream and laugh like idiots, and drive around for hours just being young. And when I was eighteen and in love with a boy, I'd scoot over in his pickup, lean my head against his shoulder, and get lost in a dream world while he ran his fingers through my hair and the two of us just drove.

I traveled many of those same roads on this particular day. A snoozing and slobbering Celia made the most of it, and even Dominic closed his eyes and drifted off for a bit. Lucy just smiled and looked out the window, no doubt dreaming the kinds of dreams that six-year-old girls dream.

An hour into our drive, I had passed the site where Jimmy and I had our accident so many years ago. I passed the cabin that I'd once upon a time dreamed of living in. And before I knew it, I was driving up the twisty roads and found myself at Mr. Clowder's place.

I looked into his pasture. The tarp was gone. Percy was gone.

I hadn't even thought about Percy today. Hadn't had time. Looking after children was a fairly all-consuming enterprise—and one that I had little experience with. Living on my own in Seattle as an investigative reporter hadn't prepared me for the domestic life. It was only afternoon, and I already wanted only to jump into bed and sleep for days.

But I knew that my day was only at intermission. And with no bed or glass of wine in sight, I instead decided to make the most of my driving time to think about the case.

The case of goat murder.

Percy was hit with a single shot just above the shoulder. The kind of shot a hunter makes. A shot meant to kill. The killer stood at the tree line, where he left a note. *Bang Bang.* Super creepy. Like in the movies.

So who could it have been?

Mr. Clowder had no ideas. Said he didn't have any enemies. But I knew from experience that people were often terrible judges of other people's opinions of them. Mr. Clowder had run a business for decades. Stuff happens in business all the time. And when money's at stake, people get mad. Sometimes mad enough to kill.

But kill a goat?

That seemed more like the type of thing a dumb teenage boy might do. But this didn't feel like the work of a teenage boy. Teenage boys are reckless and stupid, and that note wasn't reckless. It was *calculated*. Left there to send a message.

Besides, I would expect a teenage boy to fire five shots into the goat's body. Not one perfectly placed kill shot.

Nope. This definitely felt like the work of a man.

I meandered on up the tree side of Moose Mountain, past the old cabins that seemed like they had existed there since the beginning of time, then finally took a turn to come back down by a different route.

I was just coming up on Old Mrs. Greeley's place when I saw it. Tucked behind the mossy stone wall that bordered her place was a large rectangular sign reading "Jenkins Real Estate." And at the top, a smaller sign read "Sold."

I knew the mayor had been trying to buy up the properties on this side of the mountain for her big new development—Sawtooth National Ski Resort—and that she'd been offering good money. But people like Mrs. Greeley had been on the mountain so long, I'd assumed that money wouldn't be enough to move most of them.

When I was little, Granny called Mrs. Greeley "the bird lady." She had probably a hundred bird feeders in her front yard, and spent most of her life tending to her flowers and watching her birds. She ran the local Audubon Society, and she even tagged and tracked some of the birds that migrated through her property.

Now the bird feeders were gone. The birds would have to fend for themselves.

And I couldn't help but wonder what sort of offers had been made on Mr. Clowder's place.

I called his number as I drove, and when he answered, he was sniffling.

"You okay, Mr. Clowder?"

"How okay can a man be when he buries his best friend?"

"We're talking about Percy, right?"

"Yes, we had a nice little service for him. John Riley, our mail carrier, came out to perform the ceremony."

"I didn't know postal workers did funerals."

"Well, I don't know if they do. But I wasn't rightly sure who else to ask to do the honors. I'm a Methodist myself, but Percy… well, there *were* times he seemed like a good Methodist goat, but other times he acted downright Catholic. And every once in a while the Baptist in him would come out. Confusing, to say the least. But he absolutely loved John. You'da thought he was a beagle the way he'd go on and on whenever the mailman showed up. In fact, in the hot summer months, Percy was rather fond of licking John's sweaty shins… so it seemed a natural fit for John to perform the ceremony."

"I suppose every goat deserves a proper sendoff," I said.

"There are one or two goats I've crossed paths with that I hope are burning in hell, but you're mostly right. Goats generally deserve better than people, and Percy more than most. John did a wonderful job, and we laid a nice wreath down. And Percy would have loved the music. Warden Bristow from the county correctional facility is an old friend of mine. He let the Cook County players come by."

"Wait—the warden let inmates out for a goat funeral?"

"How else would I get the best polka players in central Idaho to play for my Percy?"

Ask a stupid question.

"Um, Mr. Clowder, I know this is a difficult time, but I do have a question for you. I just saw that Mrs. Greeley is selling her place. Sold it, actually. Did you know about that?"

"Found out last week."

"And has the mayor approached you about selling your cabin?"

"Oh, sure. She's approached all of us. Then last week, a different woman showed up."

"She works for Mayor Jenkins?"

"I don't rightly know. She called herself an independent real estate consultant, whatever that is."

"What did she want?"

"The same—to buy my property. Told her the same thing I've told the mayor. Not interested. Not for twice market rate. Not for any amount of money. That woman was insistent. She said with the amount of money she was offering, I could build a home anywhere I wanted. I laughed right in her face. I told her I already lived where I wanted.

The mountain's my home."

"And how did she take that?"

"She was angry. I got the sense she's not a woman who hears *no* very much."

"Mr. Clowder, why didn't you tell me about her when I asked you about enemies?"

"Enemies? She's just a woman I said no to. I don't even know her. That doesn't count as an enemy in my book."

"What was this woman's name?"

"Jones."

"Does she have a first name?"

"I presume she does, but I don't know it. She shook my hand like she was wielding a bayonet and told me her name was Ms. Jones. Hope... you don't think this Ms. Jones had something to do with my Percy, do you?"

"I'm just trying to consider anything that might provide a motive for someone to murder a goat. What did this Ms. Jones look like?"

"Tall. Blonde. Pretty... I guess. Wore nice clothes."

"Nice how?"

"Like she was going to a business meeting."

"Could you pick her out if you saw her?"

"Probably. Especially if I saw her eyes. They were strange."

"Was there something special about her eyes?"

"Just that they never blinked. And they were gray."

"Gray isn't exactly what I'd call strange. I've seen gray eyes before."

"Not like these, Hope. They were a gray like you've never seen in your life. A cold gray. And they were lifeless."

✎ CHAPTER NINE ✎

We had frozen pizzas and juice boxes for dinner. It was glorious. Except for the part where Dominic handcuffed my ankle to the kitchen chair. And the part where me and my kitchen chair chased him around the house while he laughed hysterically. And the part where I finally caught him, and he laughed so hard he started to pee.

Other than that though… glorious.

When I got the handcuff key from him—and I only barely stopped him from swallowing it—I not only unlocked the handcuff from my ankle, I also handcuffed Dominic's hand to his foot. That made Lucy laugh so hard she started to pee. It was worth it.

Eventually I unlocked Dominic and got everyone clean clothes, and then the four of us sat on the couch with some popcorn and binge-watched *SpongeBob SquarePants*. Dominic kept wanting to switch it to *The Walking Dead*, but Lucy and I threatened to watch *Downton Abbey* and he quickly agreed that *SpongeBob* was a pretty good compromise.

I rocked Celia to sleep, then tried to tiptoe past Lucy and

Dominic's room so I could go downstairs and pour myself a glass of wine. But these kids were on the lookout. Before I even reached their doorway, they yelled "We want a story!" in unison.

And not just any story. They wanted a genuine *made-up* bedtime story.

I tried to pretend I was making up, on the spot, a story about this kid named Peter Parker who was bitten by a radioactive spider. They didn't fall for it. I'd forgotten we'd just read three Spider-Man books the night before.

"Fine. What kind of story do you want me to make up?" I asked.

Dominic smiled. "How about one where that old dead arm I found comes back to life and terrorizes an entire village!"

I knew doing that would land me in the Most Irresponsible Babysitters Hall of Fame. But then again, I've always wanted to be in a Hall of Fame, and when Lucy said she was okay with that story, I figured… what the hell.

I called the story: "Godzilla Versus Dominic's Old Dead Arm." It was set in the city of Tokyo, 1975. And despite Godzilla's ability to breathe fire and his fifty-foot stature, in the end, Dominic's old dead arm was able to stop him… and save the people of Tokyo.

When I finished, Lucy clapped. But Dominic had tears in his eyes.

Uh-oh.

"Was it too scary?" I asked.

Dominic shook his head. "That's the best story I've ever heard!" He flung his arms around my neck and squeezed.

"Thanks, Aunt Hope. I promise not to handcuff you to anything tomorrow."

I said prayers with the kids, then went downstairs. Finally, I was alone. I'd never before realized just how great being alone could be.

I checked the DVR for something brainless and a little trashy. Katie did not disappoint. They'd taped one of her favorite shows, *Bachelor in Buffalo*. That would do nicely.

I was headed to the kitchen for a bottle of red wine when the doorbell rang.

"Who on earth?"

I jogged to the door with my hairs standing on end. I'd lived by myself for years and had never been frightened by a doorbell, but now that I was the protector of these little animals, it made me nervous. I looked through the peephole, and what I saw made me nervous in a whole different way.

Cowboy boots, blue jeans, long brown coat, gold star, cowboy hat, and piercing green eyes.

I opened the door. "Alex? What are you doing here?"

He gave me a nervous smile. "I knew you were alone watching Katie's kids."

And…? I wanted to ask. But I said nothing. I matched his awkward silence with an awkward silence of my own.

Finally he raised a brown paper bag and shrugged. "So I grabbed some chocolate cake. I thought maybe after finding another dead body, you might want some company?"

"I'll have you know that I just told a bedtime story called 'Godzilla Versus Dominic's Old Dead Arm,' so I think I'll be all right."

His face fell. "Oh. Yeah, no, I didn't mean…"

I grabbed the paper bag. "But I would *love* some chocolate cake. Come on in."

Alex stepped inside, took off his hat, and looked around. His smile was back, but not a big toothy grin. This one was relaxed and subtle and it called attention to the little dimple at the corner of his mouth. Sheriff Pain-in-the-Butt Kramer was off-duty. The guy who gave me butterflies was on the clock.

"I hope you don't mind me dropping by unannounced."

"Mind?" I said, my voice cracking and the breath catching in my chest. "Not at all. I was just pouring myself a glass of wine and saying to myself, 'I sure wish someone would drop by unannounced with a piece of chocolate cake.' And here you are."

"And here I am."

"Well, uh… the living room's right there. I'll, uh… be right back."

I went into the bathroom and locked the door behind me. Taking a deep breath. I looked in the mirror. What I saw looking back at me was a character straight out of "Godzilla Versus Dominic's Old Dead Arm." I smelled my pits. They, too, were straight out of the story. The dead arm part.

I worked as quickly as I could. Splashed water on my face. Put deodorant on over my shirt. Brushed my teeth… then regretted brushing my teeth, knowing that I was about to have wine and chocolate. *Arggh!* Maybe I *didn't* like it when hot guys dropped by unannounced.

I hustled into the kitchen, poured two glasses of red wine, drank one of them quickly, then poured another glass.

That's when I heard a very strange sound.

Is that... a vacuum?

I grabbed both glasses and went to the living room, where Alex had cleaned up all the toys, picked up the plates from dinner, and was now vacuuming the carpet. He turned it off just as I entered.

"I'm not sure how to feel about this," I said. "Don't tell me you're some kind of neat freak."

He shook his head. "Not a neat freak. Not a slob either... but definitely not a neat freak."

"Then what's with the Felix treatment?"

His eyes widened. "From *The Odd Couple*. Nice reference. Listen, I can't imagine watching Katie's kids for two days."

"And by Katie's kids, you mean Dominic."

"He let the air out of my tires once."

"He handcuffed me to my chair."

Alex laughed. "And since you did find another dead body today... I thought picking up some popcorn and vacuuming was the least I could do."

He finished vacuuming the last few strips of carpet, then I handed him his glass of wine and we sat down on the couch. He took two black Styrofoam containers from his paper bag and opened them up.

"For you, Madame, I have a piece of Mazzarelli's Death by Chocolate cake, some fresh whipped cream, and one fancy plastic fork."

I cut away a corner of the cake, dipped it into the whipped cream, and stuffed it into my mouth.

"Oh, my mother…"

He was watching me, apparently enjoying this. "That's a good thing?"

"My mother's not a good thing. But this cake… wow. Thank you."

"You're welcome."

He took his first bite, and had a very similar reaction to mine. "Oh my mother is right."

I pulled up *Bachelor in Buffalo* on the DVR, and it was every bit as ridiculous and awesome as I had hoped. Alex and I ate our cake and drank our wine while we laughed at the show. But when the show ended, I found myself looking at Alex, wondering about this man who had found his way to my weird little town and somehow into my weird little life.

"What?" he said.

"I feel like you know a lot more about me than I know about you."

"I don't know about that. You know I grew up in Salmon. Wanted to be a cop. My folks are gone. And now I'm here."

"Wow. I stand corrected. Five whole sentences. Practically an autobiography. I'm serious, Alex."

He leaned over in a way that made me nervous. "If you were serious, this wine glass wouldn't be empty."

"Pay to play?"

He winked. "Something like that."

I went to the kitchen, veered to the bathroom again, and did another pit check. They definitely didn't smell good. But hey, maybe his pits didn't smell good either? Maybe our pits would cancel out?

I checked the rest of me in the mirror. It would take a lot more than a splash of water to bring this up to grade. I would have to rely on the wine. And lighting.

I took the wine back to the living room, turned the lights down a bit, poured us each another glass, and tucked my feet under me as I cozied onto the couch.

"So what do you want to know?" he asked.

"You told me about your parents. I don't remember any mention of siblings."

"I've got an older sister. Shelly. Married with three children. Lives in Denver."

"And you and Shelly get along?"

"Of course."

"And her kids?"

"Two boys and a girl. I see them three or four times a year. This is easy. Anything else?"

"Anything?"

He paused. "Almost anything."

"Have you ever had to shoot anyone?"

His face fell.

"You have?"

He nodded soberly.

"More than one?"

He nodded soberly again.

"Wow... I'm sorry."

"Don't be. I'm lucky. I know that I stopped bad people. Really bad people. I rest easy."

We went back to sipping our wine.

"Favorite color?" I asked.

"Yet another hard-hitting question."

I laughed. Then grew deadly serious. "Pretty evasive on the whole color question."

He narrowed his eyes. "Because I don't have one."

I threw a pillow at him. "Liar! Okay, let's stop messing around. Favorite movie?"

"*Shawshank Redemption*?"

"Good choice. How about a food everyone loves that you can't stand?"

"Pumpkin pie."

"What? Pumpkin pie's almost as American as apple pie!"

"It's got a weird texture. Like I'm swallowing my own tongue."

"Okay, weirdo. Pumpkin pie aversion noted. Hmm... CNN or Fox?"

"Barbecue," he said firmly.

"What do you mean?"

He shrugged. "I'd rather sit down with people over barbecue and beer and talk things out."

"Thought that was going to be another weird answer... turned out good. Now for the tough one."

He took a long sip of his wine. "Give me your best shot, Walker."

There was one thing I was particularly interested in knowing. When he wasn't being Sheriff Kramer, the lawman who got annoyed with me for being better at solving murders than he was... when he was just sitting around

70

being little ol' Alex... did he think about me?

And if he did, what did he think?

But I couldn't possibly ask that. First, because that would be the kind of honest that people call "desperate"—and I had entirely too much pride to ever let someone see me being desperate. And second, because I was hoping that him showing up tonight with chocolate cake had already answered my question.

But there was something else I was interested to know. How did I guy like Alex Kramer make it this long without being... well, already attached?

"You've got nothing else?" he asked.

I was a professional investigative journalist. I was willing to walk right up to a mob boss and ask him about his business. But talking to this nice man who sat a mere two feet away from me, sipping wine... this was hard.

Just do it, Hope.

"Have you ever been in a serious relationship?"

He stopped his wine glass midflight. "You mean, with a..."

"Girl, Alex. Have you ever been in a serious relationship with a girl?"

"Ahhh, a girl." He took his sip. "Define serious."

"Now you're messing with me. Serious. You know, ever been married? Been close to being married? Have you ever been in love?"

I said that last part a little more aggressively than I'd intended. I shrank back into the couch while Alex mulled the question over, like he was working figures in his head.

Which made no sense to me. It was a pretty simple question.

Then, without warning, he smiled one of those make-me-go-wobbly smiles, scooted closer to me, and started to lean in.

I didn't know what I was expecting—but I was not expecting *that*. My heart tried to leap out of my chest, and I found myself shaking.

And that's when his phone rang. It caught me so off guard that I jumped and spilled my remaining wine down the front of my shirt.

Alex fumbled for his phone, then answered. "This is Sheriff Kramer." A long pause. "Are you certain?" He shot me a glance. Then: "Sure, I'll be right there."

He stood up and shook his head.

"That went much faster than I figured. That was Dr. Bridges. They got a dental match, and Bubba and Mary were right. Positive ID. That corpse you found was Wanda Wegman."

"And you have to go *now*?"

He put his cowboy hat on and shrugged. "Well, Dr. Bridges found something else, and I'd better get started on it."

"Started on what?"

"My investigation. Dr. Bridges found evidence that tells us this definitely wasn't an accident. Wanda Wegman was murdered."

~ CHAPTER TEN ~

Dominic woke me up the next morning with a gentle technique I like to call Jumping on Aunt Hope's Face. What made that experience even more enjoyable was the solid ten or fifteen minutes of sleep I'd enjoyed before the human alarm clock attacked me.

To say it was a bad night's sleep would be an understatement.

It felt like I spent the entire night replaying the strange events of the day in my head. I, Hope Walker, had basically been mom to three kids for an entire day. Okay, sure, I'd also spent part of the day following up on a goat murder, and of course there was the small matter of unearthing a human skeleton. But despite all of that, I had survived—and more importantly, so had the children.

And then, who should appear at my door but Sheriff Kramer? Not to complain about how I was getting in his way. In fact, he didn't come as "Sheriff Kramer" at all. He and his brilliant green eyes and his smile that made me go weak… they came as Alex.

Oh, and let's not forget the chocolate cake.

It was hard to believe, looking back on it, that we'd just sat on the couch eating cake and drinking wine and laughing at the TV like normal people. It had been so long since I'd done that, I'd forgotten how good it felt.

And then he'd leaned in.

That had caught me off guard... in the best possible way.

A cute guy shows up at your door with late-night chocolate cake? I suppose most women would consider that a sign. Especially if that woman was a professional investigator. But after Jimmy's accident, I closed that part of myself off, and for a decade now, all I'd done was work. As if by working hard enough, and well enough, and long enough, then maybe, just maybe, the pain would go away.

But now I'd returned to Hopeless. To people I cared about. To Granny, and Katie. And along the way I met this incredibly handsome—and infuriating—man.

And he leaned in.

I think I know what was going to happen. I mean, he showed up at my house with chocolate cake, right?

But I wasn't sure.

Stupid Dr. Bridges. Why did he have to choose that moment to call? It was a Saturday night! Can't murder investigations wait until Sunday?

Unless...

What if it *wasn't* Dr. Bridges? What if Alex was lying? Maybe he'd actually given someone a signal. *Hey, if it's going really bad, I'll lean in, and then you call and I'll pretend I have work to do.*

Maybe he leaned in and saw a big chunk of chocolate

cake in my teeth and he gagged. Or worse, maybe he leaned in and got a whiff of my pits.

Maybe the pits didn't cancel out after all.

Argghhh!

Back and forth and around in circles my brain went. Until finally, somewhere in the wee hours of the morning, the neurons in my brain stopped firing and I fell asleep. Only to be awoken by a five-year-old's knees ten minutes later.

Thanks for that, Dominic. I still prefer you to stupid Dr. Bridges.

I grabbed Celia from her crib and stumbled downstairs to the coffeemaker. Dominic disappeared, no doubt to plot something nefarious. Lucy wasn't around either—probably reading a book.

According to Katie's schedule, the kids usually ate pancakes and sausages and eggs on Sundays, but the chances of that happening were about the same as the chances of me making pancakes and sausages and eggs on a Sunday.

I put two bowls of cereal out for Lucy and Dominic and yelled for them to eat their breakfast. Then I strapped Celia into her high chair and started feeding her. I kept my eyes open just wide enough to make sure I was still feeding a human child. I was hoping if I kept my eyes half closed, maybe I could get something close to half sleep.

To my surprise, Dominic was not plotting my untimely death. In fact, he and Lucy had been orchestrating an even bigger surprise. When they ran down the stairs and presented themselves before me, they looked great. Lucy was wearing a long blue dress with a pretty white bow, and Dominic was wearing long corduroy pants, a button-down shirt, and a tie.

Maybe I really was asleep. This had to be a dream.

"Are you two distracting me while some kind of deadly creature wraps itself around my neck?"

"Even better!" Dominic said.

"Yep!" said Lucy. "We're ready for church!"

"Church?" I said. "You guys go to church on Sundays?"

"Silly Aunt Hope," said Lucy. "Everybody goes to church on Sundays."

I had to respectfully disagree. "Everybody does *not* go to church on Sundays," I said as I shoveled another bite of rice cereal into Celia's big chubby cheeks.

"Granny and Bess are always there," Lucy said.

"And Pastor Lief is there," Dominic added.

Lucy giggled. "He *has* to be there. The mayor's usually there too."

"Well that's not going to make me run to church."

Lucy smiled. "There's someone else who's usually at church." She looked at Dominic, and the two of them giggled. "Sheriff Kramer."

I stopped the spoon just as it was about to hit Celia's lips. "Sheriff Kramer goes to church?"

"Mm-hmm," said Lucy.

"And what time does church start exactly?"

Lucy looked up at the clock. "Thirty minutes."

I jumped up from my seat. "Hurry up, kids! We're going to church!"

~ ❦ ~

When my life's story is written, I hope there's a special chapter for that time I thought I could take three children to church by myself. This is probably why God made it so people normally have children one at a time instead of as litters. Dogs can have litters, because they never have to change diapers during church. Dogs don't have to keep their giggling children quiet during Pastor Leif's sermon. And dogs definitely do not have to confiscate a straw from a five-year-old boy who's just launched a gigantic spit wad at the mayor of Dog Town.

There were many other eventful things crammed into that service, but if I mention them all it'll feel like I'm just showing off.

I'd love to say that getting to see Sheriff Kramer made everything worth it. But having the guy you like see you act like a complete spaz for an hour straight isn't my idea of modern courtship.

When the service finally ended, Granny was laughing so hard I thought her teeth might fly out of her mouth. And two people were headed directly for me. Mayor Wilma Jenkins and Sheriff Alex Kramer.

Unfortunately, Wilma got to me first.

"I bet you put that little creep up to that, didn't you?"

"For your information, Wilma, Dominic is not a creep. He's more like a psychopath—like the kind of people you do business with. Also, if *I* had been behind it, he wouldn't have launched a spitball at your head—it would have been a rock."

"That sounds like a threat."

"What good would a threat do to a woman backed by Tommy Medola?"

Wilma stepped closer. "I do not need a man backing me."

"Hey, I saw you finally got someone to sell on the tree side of Moose Mountain. You make Mrs. Greeley 'an offer she couldn't refuse'?"

Wilma frowned. "A generous offer. We made Mrs. Greeley a generous offer. And she accepted. Nothing more and nothing less."

"I heard Mr. Clowder and the rest aren't too keen on selling. That throws a wrench in your plans."

"They'll come around. You can't fight progress. With a name like Hope, one would think you'd understand that." She glanced over her shoulder and saw Sheriff Kramer waiting to speak to me, then looked at me with a little twinkle in her eye. "I see..."

As Mayor Jenkins waltzed away, Sheriff Kramer took her place.

I had a cherubic child plastered to my hip, several wet spots on my chest where Celia had used my top as a binky, and a five-year-old standing beside me, looking for targets to take out with a loaded straw. I was a mess. But it was good to see Alex.

"Morning, Sheriff."

He pointed at the children. "I recognized these three faces, but I don't believe I've seen the likes of you around these parts, Ms. Walker."

"These parts being church?"

He smiled. "Indeed. Hey, listen, about last night…"

"Yes?"

"I just… I wanted to say sorry for dropping in unannounced like that."

"You're… sorry?"

"I didn't mean it like that. Just, I'm not sorry about dropping by."

"Good."

"But I am sorry that I had to leave when I did."

Me too. "I guess murder investigations trump *Bachelor in Buffalo.*"

"I think Dr. Bridges was pretty excited he found something on his own."

"What exactly did he find that was evidence of a murder?"

"Lucy!" whispered Dominic loudly. "Aunt Hope just said 'murder' in church."

Lucy and Dominic looked up at me with wide eyes.

"Am I not supposed to talk about murder in church?" I asked.

Lucy leaned over to Dominic. "Maybe she'd know the rules better if she came more often."

Alex smiled. "From the mouths of babes."

I glared at him. "Shut up."

"You're not supposed to say 'shut up' in church either," said Dominic. "You're really bad at these rules."

"Perhaps we should step outside where there are fewer rules?" Alex suggested.

I hustled the little animals outside onto the sidewalk, and

Alex stopped beside me, rocking back and forth on his cowboy boots.

"So…" I said. "You have big plans today?"

"Big murder investigation plans."

"Those are my favorite kind. Too bad I'm watching children all day."

"You'd rather be investigating a murder than taking care of adorable children."

I leaned in. "I know that sounds super terrible… but yes, I really would."

He put his cowboy hat on and smiled. "Well, duty calls."

"You didn't answer my question."

"Last night?"

"Oh, well… um… I meant, what did Dr. Bridges find? Why's he so sure it's murder."

"Oh. Well, once he got all the dirt cleared away, he found a broken knife blade stuck between her third and fourth ribs."

"She was stabbed?"

"It appears so. But I suppose that's for the sheriff to find out." He tipped his hat. "Enjoy your babysitting, Ms. Walker."

"Enjoy your murder investigation, Mr. Kramer."

As he climbed into his pickup truck and drove off toward Bubba's, I was sad to see him go. I was also sad he got to go ask people questions about the murder, and I didn't. Did that make me a bad person? Almost certainly.

Time to double down on that bad person thing.

"Kids, raise your hands if you're hungry!"

Lucy's and Dominic's hands shot into the air.

"Perfect," I said as I turned my little crew toward Buck's Diner. "Because I've got just the place to go. And if we're lucky, maybe we'll get to start our *own* murder investigation."

~⊙ CHAPTER ELEVEN ⊙~

The children and I found Granny holding court at the big table in the middle of Buck's Diner. As usual, she was wearing her bright blue Boise State Football sweatshirt. Bess sat on her left, wearing a long gray dress, and Zeke Roberson was on her right, in khakis and a blue jacket. Flo from the hair salon was there too of course, and Buck hovered over all of them, dishtowel slung over his shoulder, filling up coffee and grabbing used plates.

But in addition to the usual crowd, there were two people at the table who weren't normally there: Stank, of Stank's Hardware, and Cup, of Cup's Cakes, the dessert business next door. Years ago, Stank and Cup had a torrid affair, and now, seeing the two of them holding hands and laughing, I knew the romance was still alive.

When Granny saw me, she stood up and started clapping. "She did it, everybody! My granddaughter not only woke up early enough on a Sunday morning to go to church, she did it with three kids in tow! Buck, do you think she could get your Medal of Honor for that?"

Word on the street was that Buck had won the Medal of Honor saving his platoon in a firefight in Vietnam, but nobody had ever seen the award, and Buck never talked about it. Today was no exception. He just laughed and poured a fresh cup of coffee for Stank.

I handed Celia to Bess, who started rocking her like she'd been doing it her whole life, then I grabbed extra chairs for Dominic and Lucy. "And to put that accomplishment in proper perspective," I said, "Dominic only shot our mayor with one spitwad during today's service."

Granny slapped the table. "He didn't!"

Dominic made a face, then got on his tiptoes and whispered in my ear.

"Correction," I said. "He shot our mayor with *two* spitwads during today's service."

The entire table howled with laughter, and Buck lost it as well. He rubbed Dominic's hair and said, "I think free pancakes for the children are in order!"

Stank objected to that. "You mean to say all this time, all I've had to do to get free pancakes was shoot Wilma in the head with a spitwad?"

The table erupted in laughter again. Dominic leaned over to Lucy and remarked, "Old people sure laugh a lot"—to which Lucy replied, "It's because they've watched *all* the episodes of *SpongeBob*."

While Lucy and Dominic started coloring on their paper placemats with the crayons Buck set out for them, I took a long, slow sip of Buck's terrible dark roasted coffee. Especially on a day like today, even Buck's coffee was better than no coffee.

Then I set my eyes on Granny. "I assume you know why I'm here?"

Granny folded her hands somberly. "But of course. We heard a body was found down at Bubba's. Which means we've got a murder to investigate." She pounded her fist on the table like it was a gavel. "Zeke, get the ketchup!"

It had become sort of a tradition that the brain trust at Buck's Diner would get the first crack at unwrapping the mystery of Hopeless's latest murder—using condiments, of course. Zeke laid the ketchup bottle on its side to represent the murder victim, and he and Flo assembled a variety of other condiments to represent potential suspects.

Buck reappeared, slid the Hangover Special in front of me, and set two plates of pancakes in front of Lucy and Dominic. I stuffed a piece of bacon in my mouth, poured maple syrup on Lucy's and Dominic's plates, and we were ready to go.

"First order of business," said Granny. "Is the rumor true? Is it Wanda?"

I nodded. "Yes. That's what Bubba and Mary thought, and now Dr. Bridges has confirmed it."

Flo made the sign of the cross and closed her eyes.

"Any chance it was an accident?" Zeke asked.

I shook my head. "She was stabbed."

Cup looked sideways at the kids. "Do you really think we should be discussing this around the children?"

Dominic and Lucy were too busy attacking their buttermilk pancakes to even look up. "I'm pretty sure they're both halfway to a sugar-induced coma by now. They're fine," I said. I took a bite of my own pancakes. "Plus, last night I told them a story called 'Godzilla Versus Dominic's Old Dead Arm,' and they slept like babies. So I don't think this kind of thing fazes them."

Flo leaned forward. "So is the other rumor true then? Did the boy really find the body?"

"He found an arm. Next to hitting the mayor in the head with spitwads, it was the greatest accomplishment of his life."

"So who are the suspects?" asked Zeke, looking anxious to start deploying the salt and pepper shakers into our crime scene re-enactment.

"I think you have to start with Bubba and Mary Riley," I said.

"No way," said Cup.

Granny raised a finger. "Cup, I know you're new to the murder investigation biz, but Hope's right. No one is off limits."

"But they knew Wanda forever," Cup protested. "The basically started the pumpkin patch together."

Buck filled Stank's coffee. "That means they really knew Wanda. And from what I remember, Wanda wasn't always the easiest woman to get along with."

I dipped my toast into my eggs and pointed it at Buck. "And Bubba and Mary guessed it was Wanda immediately," I added.

Granny nodded. "Okay, Zeke, Bubba and Mary Riley are the first two suspects. Do the honors."

With a smile, Zeke moved the salt and pepper into position.

"Okay, who else would be a suspect?" I asked.

Cup shrugged. "Wanda didn't spend much time in town. She lived at the pumpkin patch, she worked at the pumpkin patch. It was her life."

Flo and Granny exchanged an odd look, then Flo said, "I agree. I would think the suspects would come from the pumpkin patch."

"That doesn't narrow it down much," said Stank. "Hundreds of people work there part- time during the fall."

"Okay," said Granny, "we need something to represent—"

Buck pointed at her. "Don't make any cracks about my meatloaf." In a previous investigation, Granny had suggested we use some of Buck's tasteless meatloaf to represent the anonymous killer.

"Fine. Then we'll just *imagine* Buck's tasteless meatloaf on the table representing any one of the hundred or so part-time employees who work at the pumpkin patch every year. But they wouldn't be my prime suspects. Buck's wrong about his meatloaf, but he's right about Wanda: she wasn't the easiest gal to get along with. The more time you spent with her, the more likely you were to murder her."

"So you suspect one of the full-time employees?" I asked.

"Exactly," said Granny.

"How about Kip Granger?" Stank said. "He's run the farm at Bubba's for years. And he can be a bit crusty at times."

"Zeke, you got anything for crusty Farmer Granger?"

Zeke dutifully cut the crust off his toast and laid it next to the salt and pepper.

"Lucinda Meadows runs Bubba's food operation," said Cup.

"Hasn't she become something of a minor celebrity for her baking?" Flo asked.

Cup rolled her eyes. "For her donuts. If you call that *baking.*"

"Oh, I had those donuts," I said. "They're really, *really* good."

Cup rolled her eyes again.

"What's with all the eye-rolling, Cup?" Granny asked. "You a fifteen-year-old girl all of a sudden?"

"It's a baking thing. you wouldn't understand."

Now it was Granny who rolled her eyes. "Zeke, find something for Lucinda Meadows."

Buck threw Zeke a half-eaten donut from a plate, and Zeke set it on the table.

"There's also Johnny Driscoll, who runs all the computers at Bubba's," Flo said. "I've done his mom's hair a few times. She's pretty weird, and I get the idea that her son is even weirder. He still lives with her, you know."

Zeke set a bottle of horseradish sauce on the table.

"What's weird about horseradish?" Buck asked.

"What's *not* weird about it?" Zeke replied. "What's in it, anyway? Horses? Radishes?"

Now that all the condiment suspects were assembled, the investigation could begin.

"Here's what we know," I said. "According to Bubba and Mary, Wanda ran off about three years ago, but they said that wasn't unusual. They admitted they often got into fights, and Wanda had run off a few times in the past. When she didn't return, they just assumed she'd left for good this time. But apparently not. Dr. Bridges found a knife blade broken off in between her ribs."

Flo pointed at Dominic, who was still deliriously slopping up Buck's buttermilk pancakes. "The boy found her in the pumpkin patch itself?"

"Yep. While the other kids were selecting pumpkins, Dominic here found some human remains."

"Then wouldn't that point to Kip Granger, the farm manager?" said Flo.

Granny stroked her chin. "So you think for some reason Farmer Granger and Wanda got into it. He stabs her in a fury, then buries her in the pumpkin patch to hide the body. I guess it makes sense."

"Does it though?" Zeke asked. "Why would he bury her right there in the pumpkin patch? He'd have to know that someday some kid rummaging through there would find the body."

"Killers do dumb things all the time," I said.

"I agree with Zeke," said Stank. "I think Kip's too smart for that."

"Oh?" said Cup. "Because he's a man?"

Stank hesitated as if caught in a trap. Then he relaxed, smiled, and said, "Precisely." He kissed Cup on the cheek, and she blushed.

"Okay," I said, "so some of you think it was Farmer Granger because the body was found in the pumpkin patch and some of you think it couldn't have *possibly* been Farmer

Granger because the body was found in the pumpkin patch. We're off to a great start. Any other theories?"

I looked around the table, but everybody had the same look on their face. Stumped. Well, except for Flo, whose mind seemed to be somewhere else altogether.

I sighed. "A lot of good Buck's Diner was with *this* murder investigation." I stood, took one last bite of my pancakes, and grabbed Celia from Bess.

"You've got to give us more than a dead body in a pumpkin field," said Granny. "We need more evidence!"

"And if I get you more evidence…"

"We'll crack this case wide open. Yesirreebob!"

I laughed. "Thank you, Granny." I kissed her on the cheek. "For paying for my breakfast today. And thanks Buck, as always. Come on, kids. Time to go make your house look presentable before your mom and dad get home."

As Dominic slid from his seat, I could see he was hiding something in his palm.

"Dominic?" I said.

"Yes, Aunt Hope."

"You can have one shot before we leave the diner. But remember to make it count."

He grinned, took the straw from his palm, held it to his lips, and let loose. A perfect paper projectile launched through the air and nailed Granny on her glasses.

Granny howled. "Why, you good-for-nothing!" A plastic cup came right for my head, and I barely ducked in time.

"Hurry up, kids!" I shouted. "She moves quick for an old lady!"

⁓☉ CHAPTER TWELVE ☉⁓

As soon as we got into the minivan, Granny came out of the diner shaking her fist and yelling. Dominic thought it was awesome. So did I. I could tell Granny wasn't angry in the least; she just knew chasing Dominic and carrying on would make it a thrill. As usual, Granny was right. We laughed all the way home.

I gotta be honest, watching Katie's kids for the weekend was not as terrible as I thought it would be. The little boogers grew on me. And I was excited to see Katie and tell her I had survived.

But I hadn't expected to see her so soon. When I arrived at Katie and Chris's house, Chris's car was parked in the driveway, and Katie was sitting on the steps out front.

She did not look happy.

I pulled Celia out of her car seat and walked tentatively toward Katie. "Hi! I didn't expect you back yet."

She grabbed Celia from my arms and gave her a kiss on the cheek. "Well, my stupid husband had a massive craft beer hangover and I had already gotten my free breakfast, so

I figured what the hell, how about I go home and surprise my children and my new old friend?"

"And you showed up and we weren't at the house and that was terribly disappointing?"

Katie leaned down and kissed Lucy on the top of the head. "No, Hope, that's not it."

"The house is a little dirtier than you expected?"

Katie glared. "Nope. It looks like someone even ran a vacuum."

"Now, Katie…"

Katie grabbed Dominic by the shoulders and stepped closer to me, her breath hot, her eyes a little scary. "Don't you 'now Katie' me."

"I can explain."

"How can you possibly explain that my five-year-old son FOUND A DEAD BODY?"

"How did you hear?"

"How did I *hear*? My boy finds a dead body and your question is *how did I hear*?"

Dominic tugged on her shirt. "No, Mama, I didn't find a dead body. I just found the arm."

Katie covered her face with her hands. "Please tell me he didn't just say that."

"Katie," I said, "I have to say I'm on Dominic's side on this one. Under the circumstances, I think finding the arm is *much* better than finding the whole body."

She snapped her head up to glare at me. "You don't get to vote on this. My son found a dead body!"

"And that word: 'body.' I mean, there was no skin or anything like that. Try 'skeleton' instead. It sounds so much better."

"Aunt Hope's right, Mama. There was no mushy stuff, just bones. It was really cool!"

Katie shook her head and muttered, "Just kill me now." Then she looked at me. "Hope, he's going to have nightmares for a year."

"I don't think that's true. He did have a nightmare the first night, but that was before he found the arm. He dreamt that Santa brought him a Barbie. But last night, *after* he found the arm, he slept like a baby. The kid's kind of weird."

"I *know* he's kind of weird, Hope, but he didn't need to go and find a dead body?"

I spread my arms, palms up. "You're acting like this is *my* fault. *I* didn't want to take the kids to the stupid pumpkin patch. *I* wanted to lie on the couch and let them watch YouTube videos all day. *You're* the one who made me take them to the pumpkin patch."

Katie glared at me. "And somehow, mysteriously, a dead body just happened to pop up where my boy was looking?"

"Just happened to? No, Katie, *I* put the human skeleton there when no one was looking—I thought it would be great fun for Dominic to find it all by himself."

Katie paused, just tapping her foot.

"Listen, Katie, I'm sorry. Nobody is sorrier than me. But it's *not my fault* that somebody killed Wanda Wegman and dumped her body in a pumpkin patch."

"Wanda? From Wanda's World? My son found Wanda's arm? Oh my god... this is getting worse with every new detail."

"Don't worry, Mama," said Lucy. "Aunt Hope's going to find who killed her."

"What are you talking about?"

"We were just at Buck's Diner eating breakfast, and they were starting the murder investigation," Lucy explained.

Katie advanced toward me.

I held up my hands. "In my defense, they were eating thick delicious pancakes and I didn't think they were listening."

Katie made the sign of the cross.

"What was that for?"

"I'm in uncharted territory. I figured it couldn't hurt." Katie let out a big breath. "Is there anything else I should know about?"

"I think that's about it. By the way, I kind of love your kids. It wasn't as terrible as I thought it would be."

"Except for the part where my son became the only kid in the history of the world to find an actual dead body in a pumpkin patch."

"Except for that. By the way, did you and Chris have fun?"

Katie sighed. "I guess. It was weird more than anything. I think you build it up in your head how great it's going to be not having to be around your kids... and then your husband goes out and tries thirty different craft beers."

"So... not quite what you'd hoped for?"

"No, not quite. I mean this dead body thing is a real bonus though. Kids, say goodbye to Aunt Hope. She's got things to do."

"You mean investigating murder, right, Mama?" Lucy said.

Katie gave me a weary look. "Why couldn't you be a dental hygienist or something boring like that?"

"'Cause then margarita night wouldn't be as fun."

I gave Celia a kiss on the cheek and Lucy a hug. Then Dominic threw his arms around me and squeezed. "You're the best babysitter I've ever had."

I felt his hand go into my pocket. "Dominic?"

"Yes?"

"Are you trying to steal my wallet?"

"I saw it in a movie Mom let me watch."

I gave Katie the stink eye. "And you say *I'm* the bad influence?"

"I'm allowed. I contributed to his genetic code." She laughed. "Despite everything that happened... thanks, Hope, for being there."

Dominic tugged on Katie's shirt.

She smiled at him. "Yes, Sweetie?"

"Can you tell Aunt Hope's story tonight?"

"What story would that be?"

"Godzilla Versus Dominic's Old Dead Arm."

"It's a surprisingly cheery story," I said.

Katie growled. "Run, Hope. Run!"

Three blocks from Katie's house, the weekend caught up to me. I felt like pulling over right then and there and taking a nap. I knew I should go home to my apartment over the

Library, get under my comforter, and binge something on Netflix until I fell asleep.

But there was this other part of me… that kept thinking about a guy. It was the same part of me that liked solving murders. And there was only one place in town could satisfy my curiosity about both.

Bubba's Pumpkin Patch.

I would just need some serious medication first.

A few minutes later, I arrived at my dispensary of choice: A Hopeless Cup, purveyor of my favorite cup of coffee. Nick, Generation Z's most annoying barista, was behind the counter today. He was tall, skinny, and wore jeans that would barely fit a broom handle. And yet somehow, the least manly man I knew was able to grow a thick Abraham Lincoln beard on his jaw.

"Hello, Nick," I said. "And if you say 'Hello old lady,' so help me God, I will crawl over this counter and pull out every single hair of that stupid beard. My name is Hope. You've served me sixty cups of coffee. My name is Hope."

Nick looked at Madeline, his Gen Z barista partner in crime. She rolled her eyes and pointed to a pamphlet. Nick grabbed it and handed it to me.

In big block letters, it read: *Do You Feel Triggered? Do You Need A Safe Space?*

"What the hell is this?" I asked.

"Madeline and I thought this might help you with whatever problems you have."

"What problems are you talking about?"

"Whatever problems turn you into an angry old woman

every time you come in here."

"For the last time! I am thirty-two years old. I am not an old woman!"

"Chill, dude! Just read the pamphlet before you come in next time. One white mocha coming up!"

In that moment, I was thankful for two things. First, that I was too tired to jump over the counter, and second, that Nick was much better at making a cup of coffee than he was at everything else in his life combined. Three minutes later, I was sipping down dollops of sweet heavenly caffeinated goodness and walking back to my car.

Mr. Clowder was just coming down Main Street in his truck. He pulled up alongside me and rolled down his window. "Hello there, Hope!"

"Hi, Mr. Clowder, what are you up to?"

"Just heading over to the hardware store for some supplies. Any chance you got any leads on Percy's murder case?"

"Sorry, Mr. Clowder. I haven't had time to do much."

"I've been thinking more about that scary Ms. Jones woman who came to talk to me."

"More like threatened you."

"Exactly. You really think a woman might be mixed up in Percy's death?"

"I don't think it has anything to do with being a woman or a man. Some people are just bad people. Did you get the feeling she was one of the bad people?"

He nodded. "I guess I just never connected the dots until you brought it up. But why do you think she might have done it?"

"Isn't it obvious? To scare you away."

Mr. Clowder shook his head in disbelief. "You really think that's it?"

"Think about it. People are making you offers for your home. From what the mayor tells me, they're 'generous' offers, and you still won't accept. So maybe someone thinks if they can make your life miserable, you'll just say the heck with it and take your money and run."

"That's horrible," said Mr. Clowder.

"Like I said: good people and bad people. You sure you haven't seen her around town at all?"

"No. I sure wish I had a picture of her. Maybe we could show it around and somebody would recognize it. Not sure the few details I remember are going to help much. I mean, I can picture her clearly… I just don't know how to describe her exactly." He shook his head. "Too bad it's not the movies where they have the police sketch artist."

I had an idea.

"You said you're heading over to Stank's Hardware?" I asked.

"Yep."

"I don't know a sketch artist… but I do know a very good artist. Her name is April, and she works for Stank. I'm headed somewhere else, but I'll call her right now so she knows you're coming."

"You think she'll help me?"

I winked at Mr. Clowder. "She owes me."

∽ CHAPTER THIRTEEN ∾

With Mr. Clowder setting off to see the closest thing Hopeless, Idaho, had to a police sketch artist, I set off in the opposite direction to find Wanda Wegman's killer.

The truth was, that was going to be a serious challenge. Based on Bubba's and Mary's statements, as well as the condition of the body, it was likely the crime had been committed three years ago. It was hard to believe there would still be any physical evidence left to be found. Witnesses, if there even were any, wouldn't remember anything. And worst of all, alibis were probably impossible to establish.

Alibi was usually a fairly efficient way of narrowing down your suspect pool. But we didn't even know for sure when Wanda died—other than "about three years ago"—and even if we did, I doubted it would help. People can remember what they were doing a week ago; nobody remembers what they were doing on a random Thursday night three years ago.

Which meant this case was going to be all about motive.

Namely, who had one. And then we were going to need to get a little lucky. The brain trust at Buck's Diner had at least helped me limit the suspects to a more manageable number. We'd decided to focus on the people who knew Wanda best: the full-time employees at Bubba's Pumpkin Patch.

It wasn't much to go on. It was nothing, really, but a guess. But as an investigative reporter, I couldn't resist. Wanda Wegman, creator of the pumpkin-chomping dragon, was found dead at her own pumpkin patch? If I couldn't find the truth, I could at least find the bones of one heck of a story.

I was trying to explain my mission to the miserable old woman selling admission tickets at Bubba's Pumpkin Patch, but she wouldn't hear it. "No ifs, ands, or buts, the cost of admission is fourteen dollars per adult."

I had already paid fourteen dollars to go to this exact same pumpkin patch yesterday. I didn't like paying it then either, but at least it was Katie's money. There was no way on earth I was going to fork over that much money to go to a pumpkin patch on business. Earl Denton had gotten better at reimbursing me for my expenses, but I had a feeling he would draw the line at pumpkin patch admission.

"What's going on, Matilda?"

The sweet voice came from my left. It was Mary Riley. She looked at me curiously.

"You're the woman who was here yesterday," she said.

I shook her hand. "Hope Walker. I'm here today with the *Hopeless News* investigating the murder. Which is what I told Matilda here."

"Oh, yes. Sheriff Kramer said you might be stopping by."

"He did, did he?"

She glanced at Matilda. "And I already told my employees to fully cooperate with you."

Matilda frowned. "But like you're always telling us, Mrs. Riley, nobody gets in free and nobody gets a discount. No ifs, ands, or buts." Clearly the old shrew was fond of that phrase. Probably had it crocheted on a pillow back home.

"I know what I usually say, Matilda, but for goodness' sake, there's been a murder. This is a little different."

Matilda sat there skeptically, her arms folded in defiance.

"Let the woman in, Matilda!" Mary shrieked, her sweet voice suddenly replaced by that of a stressed-out woman nearing the back end of middle age.

Matilda, the most charming woman in America, scowled mightily, hacked something into the back of her throat, stamped my hand, and let me go to the turnstile.

Mary met me on the other side. "I'm sorry about that. Nobody's really themselves since we got the news."

"So Matilda's normally sweet and reasonable?"

Mary laughed. "It's hard to find enough temporary employees for the season. We do the best we can."

I walked with Mary through the main entrance to the park, a tunnel made of stacks of hay bales and filled with pumpkins. At the end of the tunnel was a gigantic wooden sign with the words *Welcome to Bubba's Pumpkin Patch. A Family Tradition Since 1990.*

Mary saw me looking at the sign. She shook her head wistfully. "Hard to believe it's really been that long."

"I used to come here when I was little."

"You belong to Granny, don't you?"

"And I've been in Portland for a long time. Yesterday was my first time back to Bubba's in I don't know how long."

Mary held her heart. "And what a way to come back. I'm so sorry you had to be part of that. And your poor children!"

"Oh, they aren't mine. I was babysitting. And to be honest, I think it's the most excitement they've had in a long time."

Mary shrugged. "Well… children are resilient. So… this is a bit unusual, isn't it? A sheriff trusting a newspaper reporter so much?"

That sounded almost like a challenge. "I've got a pretty good track record. And I've got a few questions for you, if I may?"

"Of course."

"Great, I'll get right to it. I'm sure the sheriff has already told you that we ID'd the body and it was Wanda—and that further, she was apparently stabbed."

"Yes, he told me. It's shocking."

"Do you have any idea who could have done this?"

"It's all I've been thinking about. Racking my brain, trying to find an answer. And I'll be honest. I can't think of anyone."

I shrugged. "That's fine—it was worth asking. But tell me about Wanda herself. All I remember of her is she was the woman who operated the mechanical pumpkin-chomping dragon at Wanda's World. She's been with you and Bubba from the beginning, is that right?"

"Almost. We operated the pumpkin patch for a season

before hiring Wanda. Actually, we owned the farm since the mid-eighties—bought it when we were young and dumb and in love. But farming in the eighties was brutal, so we looked for other ways to make money off the land. We tried a little bit of everything until Bubba finally thought about trying a pumpkin patch. And that first year, that's all it was. A pumpkin patch with one truck giving hayrack rides. We passed out free hot chocolate and ate s'mores around a fire. It's incredible to think that all of this started off so small. But it did."

"So what happened to make it into… this?" I gestured to the theme park that now surrounded us.

"I guess you could say Wanda happened. Business was good enough that first year that Bubba was thinking of doubling the size of the pumpkin patch. But he got to talking to this woman, Wanda Wegman, and she said that was the wrong plan. She said he should start building special exhibits. Bubba had no idea what she meant, but he had a good feeling about her. So he hired her on, and she got to work.

"And of course, the first thing she did was build that crazy, amazing, pumpkin-chomping dragon. It was incredible. She said she'd grown up fixing her dad's tractors on the farm, but in addition to that she was clearly some kind of mechanical genius. Understood hydraulics and other things I don't understand. And that dragon was a *huge* hit with the kids. That year people who didn't even want a pumpkin came by just to see the dragon."

"That was the main attraction for me when I was a kid."

"I'm sure it was. It's a bit overshadowed now, but it's still a draw."

"And that's how Bubba's Pumpkin Patch became a big business?"

"Well, sort of. We were young and stupid and totally unprepared. For a good many years we charged too little and made next to nothing. But Bubba had seen the future... and he got pumpkin patch fever. What you see today is his vision. He started dreaming up all these crazy exhibits, and he let Wanda build up Wanda's World, and the rest, as they say, is history. A difficult history—but history nonetheless."

"How difficult?"

Mary's face grew weary. "Honestly? Very difficult. Heck, if Bubba had his way, he'd still charge people a dollar to get in. He's a dreamer... and I could never do what he does. But he's not a businessperson. His dreams were usually bigger than our business could financially sustain. And even though we were growing in size, the money part of it was touch and go for... well, for a very long time."

"What changed?"

She shrugged. "They say most new businesses fold within the first few years. It takes a while to figure everything out. But we survived, somehow, and eventually, around five years ago... everything kind of came together. It was kind of a miracle."

"So if Bubba's not a businessman, I take it you must be?"

"I didn't have a choice. Business is hard—especially something as odd as all this. But I learned."

"And Wanda stuck around the whole time? Up until..."

"Oh yes. Stayed here, worked here, lived here. We set her up in a one-bedroom cottage behind Wanda's World."

"Anyone live in her cottage now?"

Mary shook her head. "Bubba and I thought she might come back someday… so we just left it."

"You think I could see it?"

Mary smiled. "I'll take you there now."

The cottage was a dull gray with black shutters and a single window box with nothing but soil and a crooked brown plant. An odd smell hit my nose as we stepped inside. Not the smell of things that were dead or rotting, but the stagnant smell of things that are neither sullied nor clean. A not-lived-in smell.

A small kitchen was connected in an open concept to a living room with a single green recliner sitting five feet from a medium-sized tv. A bookcase sat against one wall, with an old set of encyclopedias filling the bottom shelf. Above that were a world atlas, a dictionary, and several books on engineering.

One corner of the living room appeared to be dedicated to holding a variety of junk. Pieces of scrap metal and wood of every shape and size. A welding mask and torch. Two huge toolboxes. Several buckets of screws and bolts and assorted things.

I looked through the scrap, trying to make sense of it. I couldn't.

"Wanda had a way of making something out of nothing," Mary said.

I went into the kitchen and checked the fridge. It was empty—and surprisingly clean.

"It started to smell after a while so we gave it a good cleaning," Mary explained.

"Did you clean the oven and the microwave, too?"

"I don't think we did," Mary said. "Wanda didn't use them much."

"She had to eat, didn't she?"

"She liked to eat out. Sometimes we had lunch together, and she almost always took leftovers home."

Next we checked the bedroom. The only pieces of furniture were a queen-sized bed, a nightstand, and a desk. The nightstand held an alarm clock and an old black-and-white picture of a woman with a small child.

"Wanda's mother," Mary said, when I looked at the photo. "And Wanda, of course, when she was a child."

I checked the desk's only drawer. It held the usual collection of miscellaneous junk: a few old pens and pencils, a pack of Post-It notes, some pennies. On top of the desk was a computer. I pointed to it. "Wanda use this much?"

Mary shook her head. "I doubt it. Wanda hated computers. Or at least, she didn't much care for Johnny's computers."

I quickly checked the bathroom—nothing of interest there either—and we returned to the living room. This had proven to be a dead end.

"I don't see anything that looks like a clue." I sighed and turned to Mary. "Which means... I don't know where to begin this investigation. If there's anything more... anything at all… you could share about Wanda, or about her interactions with others, it would be really helpful."

"Like what, exactly?"

"Well… I know it's uncomfortable to think about who might have had a reason to kill somebody. So think about it differently. Was there anyone who didn't get along with her?"

Mary ran her hands through her hair. She was clearly uncomfortable with the question.

"Okay, Mary. Yesterday when we found the body and you and Bubba were first talking, the two of you mentioned that Wanda had run off before."

"Yeah, a few times."

"Bubba said something about Wanda getting mad. About what?"

Mary started to answer, then stopped herself. "Oh, oh you think… no… I'm not doing this."

"Mary, we've got nothing to go on here."

"And I'm not going to give you any ammunition to go after my husband."

"So the arguments were between Wanda and Bubba?"

Mary chewed her lip. "It's not what you think."

I reached out and gently grabbed her wrist. "Mary, I honestly am not thinking anything. You know how often my granny and I argue? If we couldn't argue, then we couldn't communicate at all. Arguing does not mean murder. But what I've found is sometimes you just need to start somewhere. If I can understand the type of person Wanda was, then maybe I'll understand why someone might have meant her harm."

Mary nodded, then sat down on a chair. "Bubba and Wanda were the passion behind this place. Both visionaries—and that meant they often sparred. Didn't see eye to eye. And when a tough call had to be made, it was Bubba who made it—because ultimately he's the owner and she's not."

"And that would upset her."

"Yes. Wanda was a genius, I'll freely admit that, and she was a proud woman. I didn't always agree with her, and I don't always agree with my husband, either. But I understood why both of them were so passionate."

"Okay, the arguments your husband and Wanda got into, from your perspective, were ordinary... let's say, artistic disagreements. Did Wanda ever get into bad arguments with anyone else around here?"

Mary nodded. "Two people come to mind. Kip Granger and Johnny Driscoll. But I don't think either of them did this."

"Care to elaborate?"

Mary stood. "Not really. But feel free to ask them yourself."

~ CHAPTER FOURTEEN ~

My feet left Wanda's cottage with every intention of going down to the pumpkin patch so the rest of me could visit with Kip Granger. But my nose was not cooperating. And the moment my nose got a smell of Lucinda's Famous Apple Donuts, it commanded my feet down Apple Donut Lane to find my little fried apple-flavored friends.

When it came to food, Bubba's Pumpkin Patch was not messing around. And although there were snack shacks and dining halls and ice cream barns scattered throughout the park, the biggest concentration of culinary offerings was along Apple Donut Lane. What Rodeo Drive is to haute couture, Apple Donut Lane is to unhealthy and delicious festival food.

Iron Mike's Turkey Legs and Aunt Kitty's Kettle Corn were on the left. Fantastic Funnel Cones and Chuck's Chicken and Waffles were on the right. There was homemade fudge, caramel apples, chili dogs, and snow cones. If you were to die and go to a heavenly place where the food was incredible and just might kill you again, Apple

Donut Lane was the spot. And the star of the show was, of course, Lucinda's Famous Apple Donuts.

The fact that the simple and humble apple donut could be first chair for this symphony of smells and tastes was no small feat, and I was excited to meet the woman behind it all.

"Is Lucinda around?" I asked the older woman with light brown hair who was working the counter.

She smiled. "Not right now, but I'm happy to take your order."

"Do you know where she is?" I asked.

"I know where apple donuts are, and I'm willing to sell you some."

"I get the hint. Three donuts please."

I handed her five bucks, and she handed me three warm donuts in a paper tray.

"And Lucinda's driving the train right now," the woman said.

"Lucinda drives trains? I thought she was a baker."

"Lucinda does a little bit of everything around here."

I bit into the first donut and made a fairly indecent noise. Then I looked back at the woman, who was smiling as if she'd seen this happen a million times. "Can you just tell me what the secret is to these donuts?"

"Sure thing." She stepped aside and pointed to the sign behind her:

Lucinda's Famous Apple Donuts… where the secret ingredient is love.

"I bet another ingredient is apples," I said.

"And donuts," she said. "But those ingredients aren't very secret."

"Well, you wrote 'love' right there on a sign, so it's not exactly a secret anymore either."

She laughed. "Touché."

I sat down at a picnic table to eat my donuts. I supposed my investigation could wait while I enjoyed my fried rings of love. I was polishing off my second donut of the day, still trying to understand how something so simple could taste so good, when my phone buzzed. It was Mr. Clowder.

"How'd everything go with April?" I asked.

"She's sort of a temperamental thing, isn't she?"

"That's why Stank calls her Little Miss Sunshine."

"I'd call her ornery, like my bucks."

"Well, the difference is, she does not like rolling around in her pee."

Mr. Clowder chuckled. "You remembered."

"It's the kinda thing a girl doesn't soon forget."

"You were right, though, she's quite the artist."

"So it worked?"

"Heck yes. The illustration she came up with scared me it's so good. I told her to take a photo and text it to you."

I opened up my text messages, and sure enough, I had one from April. It was a photo of her drawing, with a simple message underneath: *Now we're even.*

I texted back: *Not even close.*

Then I opened up the image. "Looking at it now, Mr. Clowder. I see what you were talking about. Beautiful but scary all at the same time."

"Then I take it you've never seen her?"

"No," I said. "I would definitely remember someone like this. Listen, I'm sure you've heard about the body found down at the pumpkin patch."

"It's the talk of the town."

"I'm a little distracted with that right now. I hope you—"

"I understand, Hope. I may be sentimental about my goats, but I'm no fool. People murder is bigger than goat murder any day. All I'd ask is that you keep your eyes open, maybe show the picture around when you've got a few extra minutes, and maybe we get lucky."

Mr. Clowder hung up and I studied the picture of our Ms. Jones while enjoying every morsel of my third donut. She had the high cheekbones of a model, but her eyes looked like they were made of stone. I thought of that psycho note left by the tree line. *Bang Bang.* Then I thought of Percy lying there in the pasture.

Did this woman do that? And if so, did that mean Mayor Wilma Jenkins was really mixed up in it?

I heard the familiar chug and whistle of the train and turned to see it coming out of the trees and slowing down to its spot at the little train depot down the street. And there was Lucinda, sitting in the engineer's seat, grinning broadly. When everyone got off, a different driver took her place, and she strode toward her shop.

I still had one bite of donut left, so I didn't get up. But when she got to the shop, the woman at the counter said something to her and pointed my way. Lucinda turned and looked at me, then her eyes widened with understanding and she walked over to me.

I stood up to shake her hand, but instead, she opened her arms wide and gave me a big hug.

"I remember you from yesterday. Sheriff Kramer said you might be stopping by."

When she released me I backed up. "The name's Hope Walker. And did the sheriff really say I would be coming by?"

Lucinda smiled. "He did, and he said I should answer any questions that you have."

"He really said that?"

Lucinda sat down and nodded. "So how can I help?"

"First of all, why on earth do those donuts taste so good? And don't tell me the secret ingredient is love."

Lucinda cackled. "Well, although we do put an awful lot of love into our food, you're right, there is more to it than that. But all I can say is, it took a *lot* of tinkering to get the recipe just right."

"I was actually hoping the secret ingredient *was* love," I said wistfully. "Or possibly rainbows."

Lucinda cackled again and tapped my hand with hers. "Although I can't tell you the secret recipe, I could show you around in the back if you'd like."

"Are there sometimes extra donut pieces lying around that nobody will ever eat?"

"Plenty of those."

I popped up from the picnic table. "Then I would definitely like."

Lucinda led me through the front of her shop toward the production kitchen in the back.

"If you don't mind me asking," I said, "with all of this going on, why do you drive the train?"

"Because driving the train is fun! I like to do a little bit of everything around the patch. I designed the corn maze the last two years. Bubba lets me run the pumpkin catapult every once in a while, and working that haunted mine is a hoot. I learned a long time ago that the better I understand every aspect of the park, the better I understand the people coming here... which helps me put together the best food experience possible. I know I'm biased, but I think you'd be hard pressed to find a better food experience than what we have here at Bubba's."

In the back of the shop, a row of women in white hair nets and purple aprons were rolling out dough by hand. They all waved to us, and Lucinda smiled and waved back. And on a wall to one side were several framed newspaper and magazine articles, and even a few awards. The largest plaque stood out. *America's Best Donut. 2014.*

I turned to Lucinda, who was beaming with pride. "You won the award for best donut in America?"

She gave me a funny look. "You didn't know?"

"You'll have to forgive me. I grew up in Hopeless, but I moved away a long time ago."

"But you're back now?"

"For a little while. And it's a good thing, or I might never have found your donuts. They're unbelievable. But how on earth did donuts from Hopeless, Idaho, get chosen as the best donut in America?"

"Simple. It was a contest. And we won."

"Now how about the more complex version?"

Lucinda laughed. "It really is that simple. But… it was also really hard. I'd heard about this contest for best food in America, and I decided that if I could make that list, it would really help put Bubba's on the map. So I worked on that donut recipe until I had it perfect. Lot of blood, sweat, and tears went into that award."

"Sounds like love really is the secret ingredient," I said.

She winked. "And it sounds more appetizing than saying the secret ingredients are blood, sweat, and tears."

Lucinda spent a few minutes taking me through the donut-making process, and yes, along the way I was able to gobble up some leftover pieces from the island of misfit donuts.

Finally, she and I sat down at her desk in a tiny back office.

"Don't suppose you know who killed Wanda Wegman," I said.

Lucinda frowned. "It's all anyone around here can talk about. It's just terrible."

"Anybody come up with a good theory?"

"It's all just guessing."

"Any guesses better than others?"

Lucinda looked toward the door, then leaned forward. "The body was found in the pumpkin patch, so naturally people are thinking it may have been Kip."

"Body's found in a farm field, so it must have been the farmer?"

"That's what people are saying. I see you're not buying it."

I shrugged. "I have no idea. It's just not a lot to go on to accuse someone of murder. People don't just murder other people. You need a reason to murder someone."

"You mean motive?"

I nodded. "What are people saying about a possible motive?"

"They're not." But Lucinda hesitated, like she was holding something back.

"But do *you* think there's a possible motive?"

She glanced at the door again and lowered her voice to a whisper. "Love."

"We still talking donuts?"

"I'm talking about Wanda and Kip."

"They were in love?"

"Once upon a time, yes. Well, I don't know if it was love or not. But they dated. A long time ago."

"Who broke it off?" I asked.

"Wanda."

"And you know this how?"

"She told me. Girl talk."

"And what, you think Kip killed her in a lover's rage?"

"I don't think that, I'm just saying, it could have happened that way. I've known Kip Granger an awfully long time. I don't think he killed her."

"Anybody else have a reason to kill her?"

"Not that I know of."

"I've heard Wanda wasn't always the easiest person to get along with."

"That's true. That woman could argue with a mirror."

"Anyone in particular?"

"Bubba, Mary, Johnny, me… we all argued with Wanda."

"About?"

"You name it. Wanda was a smart woman, I'll give her that. The problem is, she thought she was the smartest woman on earth."

"She liked to give her opinion about things?"

"She'd tell Bubba what exhibit to build next, she'd tell Mary how to merchandise the goods, and she'd tell me how to improve my food."

"What did she and Johnny argue about?"

"Mostly which was better: Wanda's World or Johnny's Corner."

"They were rivals?"

"In a way. Wanda's World is full of old-school animatronics and hydraulics. Johnny's Corner is all computerized. Jazz versus rock and roll. Different generations, different styles."

"So Johnny was a rival…"

Lucinda shook her head. "But not a killer." She stood up and checked her watch. "Fifteen minutes to close and I still have lots to do."

"You're closing? But it's still early."

"Sunday's the only day during the season that we close early. Bubba and Mary want people to get home for supper on Sunday." She winked. "I'll tell Beatrice to pack up a few donuts that you can have for breakfast tomorrow morning."

"Or dessert tonight."

"Ha!" Lucinda hesitated. "Listen, Hope. I just have a real hard time imagining *anybody* around here killing Wanda, no matter how mad she made them. You want to know what I really think happened? Probably some drifter. Some psycho. A person who came and went. And if that's the case, then I don't think we'll ever really know the truth."

∽ CHAPTER FIFTEEN ∽

After a five-minute walk through a dirt-and-gravel parking lot full of strollers and red wagons and crying children, I found a tall, good-looking sheriff pacing beside my car.

"Thank you," I said.

"For what?"

"For encouraging people to cooperate."

"I thought you'd be chomping at the bit to come out here and ask some questions."

"You've been here all day?"

"I talked to as many people as I possibly could. You?"

"Only talked to a couple," I said.

"Care to exchange notes over margaritas?"

"What are you thinking?"

"You want to have dinner at the Taco House and talk about the case?"

"Tonight?"

He shook his head. "Now."

"Now? Alex, I'm a total mess."

He smiled an easy smile. "You look fine."

In this situation, "fine" was the same as a total mess. If I was going to dinner with Alex Kramer, I didn't want to look just *fine*.

"No, seriously, I'm a mess."

"I understand. Maybe some other time."

"No, that's not what I mean. I want to… can you give me an hour?"

"My stomach's going to be really hungry in an hour."

I grabbed a donut out of my to-go tray and stuffed it in his mouth. "One hour."

You know the movies where the woman takes a shower, does her hair and nails, and tries out fifty outfits all in a one-minute montage set to music? That was pretty much me. And when I got to the Taco House, I took one last look in the rearview mirror. Not bad.

If Alex said I looked "fine," I would punch him in the throat.

I found him already seated at a pub table hugging the far side of the restaurant near the old jukebox. A pitcher of margaritas and two glasses sat in front of him.

When he saw me, he did a double take. And on the second look, his eyes widened and he stood. He didn't say "fine." Instead, I could see his mouth forming a different word.

Wow.

"Wow" was more what I was looking for.

He fumbled awkwardly around to pull out my barstool for me, then pushed it back as I sat back down.

I was nervous, so I downed half a margarita right away.

He laughed. Then he looked at me again. And not the way a sheriff looks at the annoying reporter who's always getting in his way. As he fixed his brilliant green eyes on my face, he looked at me that *other* way.

Finally he smiled and shook his head.

"What?" I said.

"Nothing. I'm just glad we're… doing this."

"And by this, you mean comparing notes."

He blushed. Which made me blush.

"Naturally," he said.

"So did you solve the murder yet?"

He made a face and sipped his margarita. "Who do you think I am?"

"A guy buying a girl dinner so he can cheat off of her investigation."

"You thought I was buying?"

We both laughed at that one.

"Any progress on your end?" he asked.

"I barely got started. To be honest, Alex, I'm not sure we're going to solve this one."

"A three-year-old murder with almost no physical evidence? This one's a layup." He shook his head. "Okay, not so much."

"Then maybe this is the time when I start blindly accusing people of doing it. That's how I usually work."

"But only if you can blame the mayor in the process." He smiled. "The Hope Walker Dictum: No matter what happens, always blame the mayor."

"The Hope Walker Dictum. I like it. Is there an Alex

Kramer Dictum I should know about?"

"Certainly. 'Tis better to work with a brilliant investigator than against."

"You think I'm brilliant?"

He didn't answer. He just smiled. Which I guess was his answer. "So, who'd you speak with?"

"Mary Riley, then I looked through Wanda's cottage and had a good chat with Lucinda Meadows. Oh, and I ate several of her famous apple donuts."

"Speaking of, don't ever give me just *one* of those donuts again."

"The first donut almost disappears, doesn't it?"

"And then all I kept thinking about was where's the second donut?"

"It's cruel. You're right. I apologize."

"Get anything good from Mary or Lucinda?"

"Did you?"

"I asked you first. Plus, you're better at this than me, remember?"

"So this is your new tactic? Flattery? Well, Alex Kramer, I'm happy to say it's working."

We both took big drinks of our margaritas. It was quiet. It reminded me of the night before. On the couch. And suddenly, the quiet made me nervous. And when I get nervous, I talk.

"Both Mary and Lucinda agree on the basics. Wanda Wegman was hard to get along with, but neither of them could imagine someone around here killing her."

"Received that same message," Alex said.

"Mary did say that Wanda argued most heatedly with Johnny Driscoll and Kip Granger. Lucinda says Wanda got in arguments with everybody. Bubba, Mary, Johnny, even her. But when I asked Lucinda if she could think of anybody who might have a reason to kill Wanda, I think I got some information."

Alex's eyes flickered. He was curious.

I leaned over the table and lowered my voice. "Apparently, once upon a time, Wanda and Kip dated. And at some point, Wanda broke it off."

"So Lucinda thinks Kip killed her as part of some lovers' quarrel?"

"Something like that. But Lucinda doesn't really believe that. What she really thinks is some drifter killed Wanda and we'll never find out the truth."

Alex ran his finger around the rim of his glass. "After today, I'm beginning to think she's right."

"You spent the whole day at the pumpkin patch—you had to come up with something."

Alex shrugged. "Mary and Lucinda pretty much told me what they told you. Though I didn't find out that detail about Wanda and Kip."

"And what about this Kip?"

"He's like any number of old farmers I've met in my life. Loves what he does. Also hates what he does. He seemed upset that Wanda was dead, so that squares with the theory of them dating at one time. When I asked him if Wanda could be difficult to get along with, he said yes. When I asked him to elaborate, he asked me why. 'Wanda was both brilliant and hard to get along with. What more do you want me to say?'"

"I wonder if Kip is right," I said.

"In what way?"

"Each person is telling us the same thing. Brilliant. Hard to get along with. But nothing worth killing for. Occam's razor: the simplest explanation is usually the right one. Maybe nobody around her did kill her."

"Somebody stabbed her and buried her in the pumpkin patch," Alex said.

"Yes, but maybe Lucinda is right, and it was some random crazy. Someone just passing through town."

"And he picks some old cantankerous pumpkin patch employee as his victim?"

I nodded. "Maybe that's exactly what happened. And if so, we're trying to find connections where there are none, because the whole terrible thing was just random."

"If you're right, and this *is* a random killing… without physical evidence, we're never going to solve this case."

"So what do we do?" I asked.

"I like this drinking margaritas line of inquiry we're currently exploring."

"If only we were to bump into some chips and salsa along the way."

Alex motioned to the waitress. "I think I can arrange that."

We spent the next hour drinking and eating and laughing. Somehow we veered away from the current impossible murder investigation to talk about things a little more personal. Alex told me more about growing up in Salmon and what it was like to go on river rafting trips with his parents or lead tourists on horseback rides. I told him a few of the getting-in-trouble-with-Sheriff-Ed-Kline stories that he hadn't yet heard.

I was with a man who made me feel a little bit of everything. Aggravated at times, to be sure. But not on this night. On this night he made me feel comfortable and nervous all at the same time.

He also made me feel wanted. For the first time since Jimmy.

When he slipped away to the restroom, I found myself thinking about the night before. Sitting on the couch. When he leaned in and…

The burst of perfume hit my nose a moment before I heard her nauseating voice.

"Hope Walker, eating all alone."

I looked up to see a woman my age. She had perfect golden blond hair, full lips, and a body that appeared to have been engineered in a laboratory. She was beautiful, in a plastic Barbie doll sort of way. On this night she was wearing ruby-red lipstick, an obscenely low-cut top, and black jeans that appeared to have been painted on. This woman had been my enemy since we were five years old.

Her name was Gemima Clark.

"No, Gemima," I said. "I am not eating alone."

She sat down on Alex's stool and leaned over the table. "I know. I saw you from the bar. You and Sheriff Kramer?

Don't tell me the two of you are dating."

I'll admit, the question caught me off guard. I didn't know how exactly to answer it. So I went with the truth.

"No, we're not dating. We're just… working on an investigation."

"Oh, thank God. I knew it couldn't be true."

"What couldn't be true?"

She laughed. "You and Alex, of course. Have you noticed how hot he is?"

I said nothing.

"I'll take that as a yes. But you're probably still in love with Jimmy, aren't you?"

I still said nothing.

"Well, you won't catch *me* pining away for some dead guy. I know that my Patrick's not coming back. I guess that's the difference between you and me. I'm just more resilient. Not to mention beautiful. Successful. You get the picture."

"Is there a point?" I said.

"To this conversation?"

"To your existence."

She laughed. "Oh, just that I'm thinking about getting back out there. I'm not getting any younger. Time to find a man I can grow with. You know, handsome, brave, stable. Someone like… someone like… Alex Kramer."

She winked at me, then popped up and skittered away before I could kill her. She walked away in that exaggerated way models do where their hips and butt sway back and forth like a pendulum. I could really use Dominic and his spitwads right about now.

Actually, that gave me an idea for my next bedtime story. "Gemima Versus Dominic's Old Dead Arm."

I was daydreaming about all the things Dominic's Old Dead Arm would do to Gemima when Alex returned to his seat.

He took one look at me and said, "Uh-oh."

"Uh-oh what?"

"When I left, you were smiling and laughing. And now… uh-oh. What's wrong?"

"Nothing. Nothing's wrong," I lied.

"In my experience, when women say nothing's wrong, it usually means something's wrong."

"And in my experience, when a woman tells you nothing is wrong, it usually means she doesn't want to talk about it."

Alex stiffened up. "Okay, I get it. Do you need to leave?"

I shook my head and downed the last of my margarita. "What I need is something stronger to drink." I caught the waitress's attention. "Jameson, neat. And make it a double."

Now Alex looked concerned. "I know you just said you don't want to talk about it… but are you sure?"

"Yes, Alex, I'm sure. But you know what I would like to talk about? Last night. On the couch. About other women. Have you ever been in a serious relationship?"

Now he was looking uncomfortable. "Why does it matter?"

"Why does it matter? Because it matters, okay? Because I'm a woman and…" I let out a sigh.

"And what?"

"And nothing."

"I don't know what just happened."

"I don't either."

I leaned back, my arms folded, angry at myself that I'd let Gemima make me so angry. When the waitress brought me my whiskey, I downed it like a shot.

Alex was clearly confused, which upset me even more. I was a woman who liked a man. I thought he liked me too. He knew about Jimmy—about what I'd been through. So if he'd been in love, if he'd thought about getting married, I wanted to know about that. Because I was feeling something with him I hadn't felt since Jimmy, and I didn't want to get hurt again. I'd left Hopeless to get away from all the hurt.

I couldn't go through that again.

"Do you want to dance?" he said.

Oh my God, men were idiots.

"I'm going to the bathroom."

I stared in the mirror and took a deep breath. *Come on, Hope, snap out of it. Gemima is not Alex's fault. Jimmy is not Alex's fault. Tell him you're sorry. Have a good night. Salvage this.*

I made up my mind. I would walk right up to Alex, grab his hand, and take him on the dance floor.

But when I stepped out of the bathroom, I saw Gemima right next to him, chatting him up. He spotted me and waved. And then Gemima turned toward me and smiled.

It was a smile I'd seen before.

She leaned over, cupped her hand behind Alex's head, and locked her lips onto his.

My heart sank to the floor. I jogged to my seat and grabbed my purse just as Alex pushed Gemima away.

Gemima licked her lips and winked at me. "It was every bit as good as I thought it would be."

Leave, Hope. Leave now.

I turned for the door because I just needed to get the hell out of there. And then she said something else. Something that made my world stop.

"Just like Jimmy."

I dropped my purse, spun around, and punched Gemima Clark as hard as I possibly could.

∼ CHAPTER SIXTEEN ∼

My right fist caught Gemima squarely on her jaw, launching her backward into the table, where she and the margarita pitcher and glasses all crashed to the floor. She screamed bloody murder while she clawed at the air with her hands like she was a drowning woman trying to swim.

Alex looked at me like I was some kind of crazy person, then he bent down, grabbed Gemima, and helped her to her feet.

She lunged at me, and I was ready with a straight right.

Lucky for Gemima, Sheriff Kramer caught her inches before I connected with her nose.

"You saw what she did!" Gemima screamed. "Everyone saw what she did! Arrest her, Sheriff! She assaulted me. Arrest her!"

"Whatever," I said. "You had it coming." I picked up my purse. I was done with Gemima Clark, and at least for tonight, I was done with Alex Kramer.

"Stop," said a commanding voice. Alex's voice.

I ignored it and kept on walking. There were footsteps

behind me, followed by another "Stop!" and a firm hand on my shoulder. "Stop, Hope. I said stop."

I spun around. "Yeah, well, here's the thing, Alex. I don't belong to you—and you're not my boyfriend."

"But I am your sheriff. Hope, you can't go around punching people in the face."

"So sue me."

"No!" screamed Gemima. "Don't sue her—*arrest* her! I want to press charges."

I laughed in her face. "Good luck with that. Listen, Alex, I'm sorry for making a scene, I really am, but I'm not sorry for punching her. Now if you don't mind, I'm going home to forget this night ever happened."

"You don't mean that."

"I do."

"Well, I'm sorry, Hope, but you can't go home."

"What? You're gonna make me apologize to her?"

"Hope, I'm the sheriff. Me and fifty other people just watched you punch Gemima. If she wants to press charges, there's really nothing I can do."

"What are you saying?"

"I'm sorry, Hope, but you have to come with me. You're under arrest."

No matter how much Gemima insisted, Alex didn't put cuffs on me. But he did perp-walk me out of the Taco House, down Main Street, and to the sheriff's office.

Neither of us said anything. There wasn't anything to say.

I did punch her. Everyone saw it.

And both Alex and I knew *why* I punched her.

I was pissed at myself for letting Gemima get to me like that. And I was embarrassed that I liked Alex so much that she could get to me with something so stupid.

Alex ushered me into his office and had me take a seat in an old wooden chair. "I have to process you, then I have to contact the judge to see when he can get you into court."

I said nothing.

"I need to take your fingerprints, Hope."

"Check the file," I said softly.

"Oh… because of Sheriff Kline. Right."

Alex rifled the file cabinet, pulled out my file, and quietly started some paperwork.

"Do I have to spend the night in jail?" I asked without looking at him.

He shrugged. "I'll call Judge Thurmond and see what he wants me to do." He spent a couple more minutes filling out the arrest form, then he dialed the number for Judge Thurmond and the two of them discussed what to do next. It didn't take long before Alex said, "I understand," followed by "Right away, Judge," and "I'll see you tomorrow."

Then he turned to me. "Word travels fast, and Granny apparently knows the drill."

"She already talked to Judge Thurmond?"

"Seems he's nursing a drink at the Library as we speak."

"And?"

"I'm to release you straightaway to Granny."

"And that's the end of it?" I said weakly.

"Not unless I can get Gemima to drop the charges. You'll be arraigned in Judge Thurmond's court tomorrow afternoon at two o'clock, at which point you'll enter a plea. You'll probably want a lawyer for that."

"I'm not getting a lawyer."

"Hope, I'd really advise you to get a lawyer."

I sat there quietly.

"If you plead not guilty, then the city prosecutor might offer you a plea deal or he might take this to trial. Do you have any questions?"

I shook my head.

"Do you have anything to say?"

I said nothing. But I raised my head and fixed my eyes on his. They were still green and brilliant, but at the moment they held no power over me. I was angry. I was embarrassed. And I wanted to leave.

The door flew open and Granny and her Boise State Football sweatshirt charged in like an old blue mama bear. She went straight for Alex. "Why the hell did you arrest my Hope?"

"Because, Granny, she punched Gemima Clark in front of me and an entire restaurant full of people."

"Sounds to me like she did a public service."

"That's not what the law says."

"Interesting. Tell me this, Sheriff Kramer: in your limited experience with my granddaughter, does she go around punching people?"

"Not that I'm aware," said Alex.

"Then it seems logical to ask the question—why would she do such a thing?"

Alex said nothing.

"I guess it makes me curious. What on earth was Gemima doing right before that moment… that would make my Hope punch her?"

Alex wilted in front of her. News travels fast in Hopeless, and of course Granny already knew the answer to her question. That's why she asked it.

I could tell by Granny's face that she was a special kind of angry tonight. And in my experience, it was not good to make Granny angry. "Good night, Sheriff Kramer," she finally said.

I stood up to follow Granny out the door, but Alex stopped me.

"Hope, you have to understand. Tonight, what you saw… it was nothing."

"Ahh. But you had to arrest me because a person can't just punch somebody else. I mean, to do so is assault, right?'

"Right," he said.

"And I'm guessing when you say it was nothing, you're talking about the part where Gemima kissed you."

"Exactly."

"You didn't ask for it. You didn't want it," I said.

"Right!" Alex agreed.

"I wonder what they call it when someone just kisses you for no reason and with no consent? I think they call that assault, don't they?"

Without waiting for a response, I turned and left.

Granny didn't even bother taking me back to my apartment at the Library. She knew better. She drove me back to her house, the house I grew up in, and I went right up to my old bedroom, fell onto the bed, covered my head with my pillow, and screamed. When I'd gotten that out of my system, I curled up into a ball and looked at the half moon that had taken up residence outside my window. I thought about Jimmy and Alex and my life back in Portland, and I thought about being back here with Granny and Katie. I thought about the guy who was interested in me for a TV show. And I thought about Gemima and how crazy she made me. I thought about punching her. I'd let her get to me. I shouldn't have punched her. Even though it felt so good.

But mostly I thought about how it made me feel to see Gemima kissing Alex. The image enraged me to a degree that surprised me; I couldn't believe that I felt that strongly about Alex.

And *that* was the part that really scared me. I wasn't ready to feel that way about Alex. To feel that way about anyone.

At some point, I realized that I was not going to fall asleep, so I went to the bathroom. Then I stumbled downstairs and found Granny sitting at the end of the couch, sound asleep, the TV still on. I looked down at her and thanked God for my grandmother. Then I turned off the TV, lay on the couch next to her, and nestled my head on her comfortable lap. I closed my eyes and whispered, "I love you, Granny."

A hand stroked my hair, making me feel like I was seven years old again. And her voice whispered, "I love you too."

~ CHAPTER SEVENTEEN ~

Granny's snoring woke me up early the next morning. I slipped out of her grasp, covered her with a blanket, and tiptoed out of her house. It had been quite a while since I'd gotten up this early, but I had no intention of going back to sleep.

I was embarrassed.

And I was mad.

So I was going to rely on the usual medication. Coffee, a shower, and work. Plenty of work.

I walked back to Main Street and found my car still parked outside the Taco House. I drove toward tourist town and waited outside A Hopeless Cup until six a.m., when the "open" sign finally clicked on.

I found Nick getting things ready behind the counter. He frowned as soon as I walked in. I was not in the mood for Nick—or anybody from Gen Z for that matter.

"White mocha latte," I said. No banter today.

I sat down in the middle of the shop to drink my coffee alone. Nick ignored me and I ignored him. Finally I got up the nerve to check my phone.

I had a single text from Alex from last night. Late last night.

Can we talk?

The answer of course was no. But he was in law enforcement—he could figure that much out on his own.

I also had a text from Mark Pendergast, the TV guy. A reminder that he'd be heading back through Hopeless on Saturday. *Definitely want to meet for dinner*, he said.

I had no idea how to respond.

Instead I clicked on April's old text, the one with her sketch of the creepy woman who'd visited Mr. Clowder. I looked at that image more closely. High cheekbones, soulless ice-gray eyes. A winning combination if I'd ever seen one. I had no idea if this woman was connected to Percy's death, but she was the only lead I had. And since I had no leads on Wanda's murder, and I *needed* to work today...

I approached the counter. "Thank you, Nick."

"For what?"

"For making a great cup of coffee."

"Is something wrong? You usually yell at me and act all hormonal."

I pinched myself so that I wouldn't lose control. "Nothing's wrong, Nick. It just occurred to me that I've never told you that before."

Nick still looked confused. Maybe even a little nervous.

I turned my phone around and showed the sketch to Nick.

He leaned forward. "What's this?"

"An illustration of a woman who's been around town

lately. You seen her?"

Nick squinted, then looked up. "Yeah, she's hot, so I definitely remember her."

"You're saying you remember her coffee order, or you actually remember her?"

"I remember her for sure. She's smoking hot."

"How many times has she been in?"

"Just once, a couple days ago."

"You don't by chance remember her name, do—"

"Ms. Jones."

"Let me get this straight. I've been in here sixty times and you still call me 'old lady'… yet this woman comes in *one* time, and you remember her name?"

"Dude, like I told you, she's hot."

If Nick the barista ever ended up dead, I'd probably have to confess based on the number of times I'd wished him harm.

"Nick, I'm working with the sheriff on a very important investigation. I'm going to leave you my number. Please do me a favor and text me if this woman comes in here again."

I wrote my number on a napkin and handed it across the counter.

"You're not going to arrest her, are you?"

"Of course not, Nick. I just want to speak with her. And don't worry. We only arrest the ugly people."

Nick smiled.

"And the really dumb ones," I said as I walked away.

I drove back to my apartment above the Library, took a shower, put my hair into a ponytail, then put on my uniform for the day. Black jeans, a simple gray top, and my brown leather jacket.

When I checked my phone again, Katie had blown it up with texts.

Arrested?

You PUNCHED Gemima?

Are you alive?

Do you need alcohol?

I'm still mad about the dead arm thing.

It really is a pretty cute story. The kids made me tell them last night.

How did it feel to punch Gemima?

Wait, you were on a date with Alex?

Call me NOW or Gemima is my new best friend!

I laughed as I read through them all. Leave it to Katie to make me smile about all of this.

I went downstairs and pulled out the phone book that Granny still kept under the bar. I flipped through until I found Driscoll. Bonnie Driscoll. That had to be Johnny's mother; Flo had mentioned that he still lived with her. I wanted to catch him before he went into work today.

The Driscolls lived in a mid-century ranch on the other side of Hopeless. It looked unkept on the outside, the way houses do after a few years of neglect. I saw lights on in the kitchen, so I knocked on the front door and waited.

A woman in her mid-fifties answered the door in a bathrobe, with a mug of coffee in her hand and a bewildered expression on her face.

"May I help you?"

"Hi, Mrs. Driscoll, my name is Hope Walker. You might know my Granny who owns the Library."

"I know Granny. You belong to her?"

"I do indeed. Anyways, I'm working for Earl Denton at the newspaper, and we're doing an article about Wanda Wegman."

"Such a shame what happened."

"I understand your son worked with her, so I was hoping I could ask him some questions."

"Yes, Johnny knew her. He's eating his waffles right now. He likes Eggos. Nothing but Eggos. Always gets mad when I buy the Walmart brand. 'Has to be Eggos, Mama,' he says. That boy is particular about his waffles." Her eyes went elsewhere and her mind seemed to drift off.

"Mrs. Driscoll?"

She snapped back to attention. "Yes, dear?"

"Johnny, is he available to speak?"

"I'll see if he's finished with his waffles."

As Mrs. Driscoll stepped back into the house, I wondered about the Driscoll family. It appeared there was no Mr. Driscoll in the picture, that Mrs. Driscoll was a little off, and that her son Johnny wanted people to leggo his Eggo.

These were the facts of the case. Hard to believe I was once a big-city reporter.

A young man approached the door with the same apprehension as his mother. "Are you the lady the sheriff said would be asking questions?"

"I am. Hope Walker's the name."

"Can we go someplace else? I don't like to bother Mother with my business."

"We can talk out here?"

He stepped onto the front stoop and walked right past me. "Let's talk in the garage."

Now I was the tentative one. I cautiously followed Johnny to a detached garage behind his mother's home. An old broken-down basketball hoop hung above a large garage door, but Johnny unlocked a separate door to the side, then entered. When I hesitated to go in after him, his head popped back out.

"You coming?"

I wished I had a Walmart-brand waffle with me just in case he tried something. But I'd probably seen worse, so I paused for a beat, then I took the red pill.

To say the inside of the garage was different from the outside would be a huge understatement. This place was like some crazy computer laboratory. Work tables lined three walls, and they were covered in computers and tools and electronic gadgets. And right in the center of the garage was some sort of robot.

"I assume you've been to Johnny's Corner?" he asked with great pride.

"Been gone from Hopeless for years. First time back at the patch was on Saturday."

"And you didn't visit Johnny's Corner?"

"Sorry. Wanda's World is pretty much the only thing I remembered."

Johnny gave me a look of disgust. "Why is it so hard for people to let go of the past? I get it—she made a scrap-metal dragon that crushes pumpkins. It's really not that cool."

"My granny would always make us sit close enough so the pumpkin juice would spray all over us."

"That's not cool. That's just gross!"

"To a little kid, those can be the same thing."

"Nonsense. We live in a computer age, and kids like computers. It's the parents who hold them back. You want to see something cool?"

"Sure," I said. I was hoping that "something cool" didn't mean "a dead body I've been keeping in the freezer."

He picked up a tablet and hit a couple buttons, and his robot came to life. It rolled forward on wheels until it came to a huge block of wood that had apparently been put there to serve as an obstacle. It bent over, its two arms came down, and it lifted itself over the wood. Then it continued.

"Pretty cool," I said.

"'Pretty cool'? Are you insane? Do you have any idea how much computing power is required to do what this robot just did?"

"More than it takes to toast an Eggo waffle?"

"Was that a joke? That was a joke, right?"

"Listen, Johnny. Sheriff Kramer and I are interviewing everyone who knew Wanda well."

"Because you think that with a few chats, you'll magically be able to solve her murder. Well, I hate to break it to you, but you won't."

"And why's that?"

He smiled. "Because whoever killed her isn't going to *tell* you. No matter how many questions you ask. And without a confession, you'll never catch the guy."

"Why do you say that?"

"Listen, lady, I'm not a dummy—as you can plainly see. Wanda ran off three years ago. If the murder took place then, there can't be much evidence left that could tie the murderer to her. You don't even know what day she was murdered, so you can't check alibis. You're out of luck."

"Did you hear how she was murdered?" I asked.

"Sheriff said she was stabbed."

"And are you sorry she's dead?"

He rolled his eyes. "As I'm sure other people have told you, Wanda and I argued. A lot. Wanda argued with everybody. I wasn't sad to see her leave the pumpkin patch."

"But are you sad that she's dead?"

"To be honest, not really. I mean, I'm *sorry* she got killed. But it doesn't really make me *sad*."

"Isn't that a little harsh?"

He shrugged.

"You say you and Wanda argued a lot. About what?"

"Haven't you been listening, lady? Wanda was an antique, and I'm the new Tesla sports car. That's what we argued about."

"Did you ever want to hurt her?"

"Now you're just insulting me."

"Can you think of anybody who did want to hurt her?"

He rolled his eyes again. "Nobody that works at the pumpkin patch."

"What about Kip Granger?"

"What, because the body was found in the field and he's the farmer? I call that intellectual laziness. Try harder."

142

"Okay, Johnny, let's try a different approach. As you've pointed out, you are clearly smarter than me. I couldn't dream of doing what you've done here in a thousand years."

"How about a million?"

"So you're *much* smarter than me. In that case, maybe you can put that intellect to use. Let's say you were in charge of the investigation. What would you do? What would you focus on? Where would you look?"

Johnny looked thoroughly annoyed. Then he rubbed his hand across his jaw. "Talking to people isn't really my strong suit."

"You don't say."

"I'm a scientist. I like science. If it were me, I would focus on the only piece of physical evidence you have."

"The body?"

He shook his head. "Rumor is, you have the murder weapon."

∼ CHAPTER EIGHTEEN ∼

Katie called as I was heading out to Mr. Clowder's place.

"I sent you a thousand text messages!"

"You sent me nine."

"Which might as well be a thousand after the news I heard. You got arrested? You punched Gemima? You were on a date with Alex?"

"And I really don't want to talk about any of it."

"And I really didn't want to push Dominic's head out of my yoohoo, but I didn't have a choice."

"This isn't anything like that."

"Hope! My son found a dead woman's arm while I was on a romantic getaway where my husband became incapacitated from IPAs. You gotta work with me here."

"I woke up early, I bought my coffee, I even took a shower. And now I'm working. That's what I'm going to do now. Work."

"And how long do you plan on working?"

"For the next ten years of my life."

"I was afraid of that."

"I don't want to talk about this."

"I know. How about you push it all deep inside you, then don't talk about it for the next twelve years?"

"You're a butthead."

"But I'm *your* butthead."

"I'm angry, Katie."

"At Alex?"

"Yes. And at Gemima. And at myself. Mostly at myself."

"Why?"

"Because I like him," I said.

"You do, don't you?"

"I did until last night."

"You do realize Gemima's the one who kissed *him*, right?"

"Yes."

"And you know she only did it for one reason, right?"

"Yes."

"Then what's the problem?"

"He arrested me, Katie! He had a chance to stand up for me in front of the whole town, and he didn't."

"Think you can forgive him?"

"I don't know. I just don't know."

"Think you can stop by tonight and tell the children a story? They miss you."

"Do they *really* miss me, or is it just nice to have somebody else put your children to bed for you?"

"A new *Bachelor in Buffalo* airs at eight thirty, and putting them to bed kind of cramps my style."

"For no greater love existed than to lay down one's life for another."

"One Sunday church service in six months and now you're quoting Scripture."

"Did you hear Dominic shot the mayor with two spitwads during Mass?"

"And remind me again, is that better or worse than accusing the mayor of double murder?"

"You're a butthead, Katie."

"But I'm your butthead, Hope. See you tonight."

Johnny was super creepy, but he was also right. We had very little to work with in this investigation, except for this one piece of physical evidence.

The murder weapon.

That's why I found myself waiting outside Dr. Bridges office when he pulled up in his cherry-red Jeep Grand Cherokee that morning. He climbed out, holding his black leather doctor's bag, and acknowledged me with a smile and a tip of his head. "Good morning, Hope. I'm guessing you didn't show up for a doctor's appointment this morning?"

"And how could you get that?"

"Because you're more like your grandmother than you know, and I think the last time she visited the doctor was when she was born."

"How about when she had my mother?"

"Well, I wasn't around back then, but I would bet that Granny delivered her baby somewhere between making breakfast and taking her liquor delivery for the day."

"Sounds like you know my Granny pretty well."

I walked with Dr. Bridges into his clinic, past the receptionist, who was already there, and back to his office. I sat down on an old leather chair while he fired up his computer.

"So…" he said, crooking his head at me. "Are the rumors true? Did you really punch Gemima Clark?"

"Unfortunately, yes."

He shook his head and chuckled. "Boy would I have liked to see that."

"What about the Hippocratic Oath?"

He pressed his fingers together. "What about it?"

"Doesn't it say 'do no harm'?"

"Yes, but that only applies to me. Doesn't mean I can't enjoy you hurting someone."

"What did Gemima ever do to you?"

"You remember my boy Henry?"

I remembered Henry Bridges. He was a year behind me in school. I hadn't thought about him in years.

"How is Henry?"

"Fine… now. But back in high school? Let's just say Gemima made life miserable for him. Do you know if anyone has video of you punching her? Henry would get a real kick out of that."

"I'm in enough trouble. I really hope there's not a video."

"And the arrest? That's true as well?"

"Unfortunately."

"You seeing Judge Thurmond today?"

"This afternoon."

Dr. Bridges danced his fingers on his big wooden desk like he was thinking of something. "Judge Thurmond and I are good friends. Go way, way back." He paused, then stopped and fixed his attention on me. "So, the case. What do you want to know?"

"Do you still have the body?"

"Nope, the FBI's pathologist picked it up yesterday afternoon."

"Best guess for time of death?"

"No guess, really. According to Sheriff Kramer, Bubba and Mary said Wanda left three years ago, and the level of decomposition I found squares with that estimate."

"I've been thinking: wouldn't a decomposing body give off a smell?"

"Oh, most definitely."

"So isn't it weird that it was sitting in that pumpkin patch for three years and nobody noticed the smell?"

He shrugged. "Maybe, maybe not. Farming can be a smelly business. The heat of organic material, manure, and then all the smells from Apple Donut Lane… And the body was buried, though not all that deep. I can't say I'm surprised that no one smelled it."

"What did you learn from the body?"

"Well, after that long, in fresh dirt, with no casket… when the earth and the water and the bugs and the worms can get to you… what's left isn't so much a body as a skeleton. But the teeth were all we needed for an ID, assuming it was Wanda, so I called Dr. Philpott and he brought Wanda's dental records over. Perfect match. Then I carefully cleaned the dirt and mud off the rest of the body, and that's when I discovered cause of death."

"She was stabbed."

He nodded. "In the intercostal space between her fourth and fifth ribs on the left side of her chest."

"And you know this because of the murder weapon."

"Weirdest thing. There was clay stuck between the ribs, and even though the handle had broken off, the screwdriver was stuck right there between the ribs."

"What screwdriver?"

"The murder weapon."

"Then where was the knife?"

"What knife?"

"Sheriff Kramer told me that you found a knife stuck between the ribs."

"He must have misspoken. It was a screwdriver. A flathead."

"Do you still have it?"

He shook his head. "That went with the FBI as well."

"Dr. Bridges, was there anything about the body or the screwdriver… anything at all that might help us with our investigation?"

"As you know, I'm not a forensic scientist. Since the murder rate in our little town has picked up a bit, I'm been trying to learn more, but if there's anything here to tell you… I'm afraid I'm not seeing it. The FBI are the experts; maybe they'll come back with something."

I checked my watch. It was still early. But I was already feeling today's two-o'clock arraignment at the courthouse bearing down on me.

Remember, Hope. Work. Just work.

Ten minutes later, I found Mr. Clowder in the middle of the pasture, pouring grain into some kind of feeding tub.

He waved when I walked up. "They mostly eat grass," he said as if I'd asked him a question. "But it's nice to add a little grain to their diet. Not too much, mind you. The grocery store has become nothing but high-fructose corn syrup, so I don't want to be adding to the problem. Plus, left to their own devices, goats would want to eat grain all day. Animals can be dumb. Then again, at least they only eat when they need to eat. Us humans, we eat for no reason at all. Sometimes when it comes to the simple stuff, we're the dumb ones."

"You seem philosophical today."

"I guess it comes from reflecting on Percy, on a good goat life well lived. So—what'd you think about that picture?"

"Pretty and scary," I said.

"That April really captured her likeness. I showed it around to a few people."

"Anyone recognize her?"

"Nope. Showed it to Stank since I was there at the hardware store. Then I showed it to Cup. Showed it to Pastor Lief, Buck, Flo. Nothing."

"Well, I found someone who recognized her. Nick, the barista at A Hopeless Cup. He knew her immediately."

Mr. Clowder stood up straight. "Really?"

"Said she came in a week ago."

"And he's sure?"

"He's sure."

"Then I didn't make her up."

"I never thought you made her up, Mr. Clowder. I'm going to stop by some of the other cabins here on the mountain, too. If she's trying to buy up property, you'd think they'd all know her."

"Hope, in case I forget to mention it, I really appreciate your help."

I smiled. "I'd love to say it's just because you're so darn charming…"

He laughed. "Oh, you mean that isn't the reason?"

"Mr. Clowder, killing a goat in cold blood…"

"It's terrible."

"It *is* terrible. But I was going to say it's also weird. And this beautiful real estate agent with eyes like cold gray ice is also weird. In my experience, people like to read about weird. I don't know what it is, Mr. Clowder, but somewhere in here, there's a story. And it's my job to find it."

⌒ CHAPTER NINETEEN ⌒

The first big snowfall of the season hadn't come yet, but I was sure it would soon. The days were getting shorter, the air chillier, and I saw smoke coming from the chimneys of most of the cabins. But I was headed for one cabin in particular: Mrs. Greeley's. The bird lady.

Halfway up the mountain, I parked beside the old moss-covered stone wall that framed her property. Mrs. Greeley was outside watering the flower baskets that hung from her front porch. I hadn't seen her since I was a kid, but I recognized her right away. I wondered if she would recognize me.

I opened her front gate and walked up the cobblestone path. As I approached, she scrunched over and squinted, her face full of worry, no sign of recognition. I guess I had changed more than she had.

I smiled as widely as I could. "Hi, Mrs. Greeley, I'm Granny's granddaughter, Hope Walker. I used to visit you and your birds when I was little."

She straightened up, and a smile formed across her

wrinkled face. "Little Hope Walker!" She stepped down to the path and gave me a warm hug. Her body was frail, and I felt like she might break if I squeezed too hard.

She stepped back and gave me a long look. Then shook her head. "It has been a long time. You're a grown woman. Come, join me on the porch."

Two old gray rocking chairs sat on the porch. Mrs. Greeley took one and I took the other. Almost instantly, a fat white cat appeared between my legs and purred. As I put my hand down to let it lean in, I looked out into Mrs. Greeley's yard, remembering all the bird feeders that had been here before.

Mrs. Greeley spoke up. "You're probably asking yourself, 'What happened to the birds?'"

I nodded.

"I wish there was a good answer. But the truth is, I got old. The wind blew and I got tired and it all just became too much."

"I'm sorry to hear it."

"Nothing to be sorry about. We all get older. Except your granny. Anyways, what on earth brings you to my front porch after all these years?"

"I'm an investigative reporter."

"I'd heard something about that. Portland?"

"Not anymore. Been back in town for a little while, helping out Earl Denton. I'm doing a story on the death of Mr. Clowder's goat."

She nodded gravely. "Percy. Mr. Clowder was fond of him. Heck, he's fond of all his goats."

"I noticed the sold sign in your yard."

"And you came to ask me why I'm selling my soul to Wilma Jenkins."

"Not sure I would phrase it quite like that."

She chuckled. "Well, I would. I can't say I really wanted to sell… but the offer was good. Like I said, I'm old. And I didn't want to bother with all of it."

"With all of what?"

"With whatever makes these cabins suddenly so valuable to Mayor Jenkins and the other real estate snakes who've been nosing around the past few months."

"There've been others?"

"Yep."

I took out my phone, pulled up April's sketch, and handed the phone to Mrs. Greeley. She pulled a pair of reading glasses out of her pocket, hung them off the end of her nose, and studied the image. Then she looked at me over the tops of her glasses.

"That's one of the real estate snakes I was talking about."

"I know."

"She was a real piece of work. Called herself Ms. Jones."

"She also visited Mr. Clowder."

"I suspect she visited everybody on this side of the mountain."

"Does she work for Wilma?"

"That wasn't my impression. She called herself an independent real estate consultant. Said she was buying up land for a motivated investor. That's what she called it, a 'motivated investor.'"

"Anything else you remember about her?"

"Well, you've got the picture right there. That's a spitting image of her by the way. She had those eyes…" Mrs. Greeley shook as if the memory gave her the willies.

"She was scary?"

"Yes. I'd have to say she was. And when Wilma called me a few days later and upped her offer, I decided, what the heck. This mountain has been my home for a long time, but things change, and you have to change with them. Maybe it's time."

"Did Ms. Jones leave you a card or a phone number?"

"Nope, she just said she'd be back. But then Wilma called, put the sold sign in my yard, and I haven't heard from or seen Ms. Jones since."

"Where do you plan to go, Mrs. Greeley? If you don't mind my asking."

"I've got a spot waiting for me at a retirement community in Boise. State of the art. Lots of bells and whistles. I'll miss Moose Mountain, but they say you make good friends there. Heck, maybe there's a couple hunks around for a little eye candy."

"Mrs. Greeley!"

She smiled. "I said I'm old—didn't say I was dead."

I spent the next two hours visiting the other cabins on the mountain. Showing everyone the picture. Hearing the exact same story every time. Ms. Jones had visited everyone, and without exception, she gave everyone the heebie-jeebies.

They'd also all heard about the shooting of Mr. Clowder's goat, and though none of them were torn up about it like Mr. Clowder was, it concerned them. The general feeling I got was that people were uneasy. And at least a few were seriously considering Wilma's latest offer.

I had time for one more visit before I needed to head back into town for my super-fun court date with Judge Thurmond. I stopped at an old A-frame log cabin with a small barn to one side and a paddock with a herd of cows on the other. A man and a woman were working in an oversized garden out front. The man was tall and thin and wore light blue jeans and a brown Carhartt jacket. The woman wore jeans and a gray hooded sweatshirt and looked sturdy and tough.

As soon as I got out of my car, the woman hollered. "We're not selling, so go away!"

"I'm not here to sell you anything," I hollered back.

"That's a load of crap!" The woman stepped toward the road. "I never seen you before, and neither has Cal." She turned back. "Have you, Cal?"

He shook his head.

"See, neither Cal or I have seen you before. So you best be on your way."

"Ma'am, my name is Hope Walker. I'm a reporter for the *Hopeless News*, and I'm working on a story."

"Good for you. Now leave us alone and be on your way."

"Mr. Clowder's goat Percy was shot."

"What's that got to do with us?"

"He thinks it's suspicious. That it might have something to do with people wanting him off his land."

The woman muttered an obscenity under her breath. Then she shook her head angrily. "I knew this was going to happen." She walked over to me, not screaming this time.

I flipped my phone around and held it out. "Have you ever seen this woman?"

The woman muttered another obscenity. This time not under her breath. "Yes, I remember this scary wench. She threatened us."

"How?"

"The way people do when they're saying one thing but meaning another."

"And did Mayor Jenkins call a few days later and increase her offer on your place?"

"As a matter of fact, that's exactly what happened. What was your name again?"

"Hope Walker."

"What the hell is going on here?"

A shot rang out from the direction of the trees, and the woman and both spun to see one of the cows in her paddock drop to the ground.

The woman took off running toward the paddock. "Cal!" she screamed."Get the gun!"

Her husband ran to their cabin.

And all I did was stand there, frozen, looking toward the trees. The smart thing to do would have been to call 911, or call Sheriff Kramer, or duck down, or get in my car and drive away, or at the very least wait for Cal and his gun.

But I did none of those things. And I didn't stay frozen for long.

I sprinted toward the trees—straight toward where I'd heard the gunshot.

The woman shouted. "Mabel's dead, Cal! She's dead!"

As soon as I reached the trees, I dropped to my knees—just like Granny had taught me to do when I was chasing a deer—closed my eyes, and listened. And I heard it: branches cracking to my right. Maybe thirty yards, maybe more.

I leapt to my feet and started sprinting, winding my way through the trees.

A minute later, I stopped again. Dropped to my knees. Closed my eyes. Listened.

Left, still thirty yards away. Heading for the ridge.

I burst forward, crashing through branches and thorns. And before I knew it, I was at the ridge, standing on the same trail that Katie and I had hiked a few weeks back, the one that descended to Patrick Crofton's cabin.

Then I noticed a yellow nylon rope attached to a tree and hanging over the edge of the ridge. I got on my hands and knees and peered over the edge. The rope hung all the way to the river. And beside the river was a red sedan. As I watched, it kicked up dirt and gravel, and it was gone.

Adrenaline takes over in situations like those. Fight or flight. But suddenly, the adrenaline wasn't enough. My body realized that it wasn't sixteen anymore, and I was not a deer. Hell, I wasn't even in shape. I stayed on my hands and knees, breathing heavily. And I realized how stupid I had been for running after the shooter.

When I'd recovered myself, I retraced my steps. Ten minutes later I emerged at the paddock. Cal and his wife were standing over their dead milk cow. The man's shotgun was in his hand.

The woman looked at me and screamed, "What is going on here?" She strode angrily toward me, her face flushed. "It's that psycho Ms. Jones, isn't it?"

"Maybe. I have no idea."

"Did you get a look at the shooter?"

"No. They had an escape route and everything. Rope hanging down the ridge. By the time I got there, the car was already pulling out."

"What kind of car?"

"Red, four-door sedan. Maybe a Chevy?"

"License plate?"

"Couldn't see it."

"Could you tell if it was a man or a woman?"

"I never saw the shooter."

The woman uttered yet another obscenity. And this time she screamed it.

∽ CHAPTER TWENTY ∾

I arrived at Judge Thurmond's court with one minute to spare. Racing through the heavy wooden doors that framed the court, I was sweaty, I was a bit scared, and I wasn't the least bit ready for whatever was about to happen.

Judge Thurmond sat straight ahead, wearing his black robe and a not terribly happy expression. To my left was Gemima Clark, adorned with the type of dark sunglasses an old lady with cataracts might have. She also had a sizeable bruise on the left side of her face.

In front of her, seated at a solid wooden table, was a severe-looking man in a dark blue suit.

To the right of him was an empty table. No man in a suit—because I had no lawyer. I quickly strode to the table and sat down.

I heard the door open behind me and turned around to see Sheriff Kramer enter the courtroom, followed by Granny and Katie. Alex avoided my eyes, but Katie and Granny both smiled and waved.

The loud crack of the gavel spun me back around.

Judge Thurmond spoke. "Would the city and the defendant please stand? In the matter of the city of Hopeless versus Hope Walker, it appears we have an assault. We also have a brand-new lawyer representing the city. Mr. Bean, on behalf of Hopeless, I welcome you to my court. Now can you please tell me what happened here?"

The man in the blue suit stood. "Thank you, Your Honor. Last night, Sunday night, Ms. Walker assaulted Ms. Gemima Clark. Ms. Walker was not defending herself. It was malicious. It was violent. And frankly, she needs to be punished."

"And what kind of sentence is the city seeking, exactly?" asked Judge Thurmond.

"Your Honor?"

"It's a simple question."

"Yes, Your Honor, but this is an arraignment, not—"

The judge banged his gavel. "Mr. Bean. I know you're new here in Hopeless, so I'm inclined to give you a little leeway. But let me make one thing clear. In my courtroom, when I ask a question, *I get an answer.*"

Mr. Bean's eyes widened. "Yes, Your Honor."

"Now. Recommended punishment?"

"Two weeks in city jail, a thousand-dollar fine, and six months' probation."

My heart fell into my stomach as Judge Thurmond nodded and turned my way.

"Ms. Walker, I understand that you are representing yourself, which, for the record, is a very stupid thing to do. Do you agree with the description of events that Mr. Bean has just provided?"

I wondered briefly what a lawyer might say. Would they object? Would they use ten words where one would do? I had no idea.

Then I thought about what Granny might do. And I went with that.

"Yes, Your Honor."

Judge Thurmond shook his head. "And that's why I really wish you had a lawyer. You agree with the city?"

"I agree that I punched Gemima in the face. Yes, Your Honor."

"So you're pleading guilty."

I shrugged. "I guess."

"You guess, or you are?"

I took a deep breath.

"I am, Your Honor."

Judge Thurmond smiled. "Good. Then we can move directly to sentencing."

Mr. Bean cleared his throat. "Your Honor? This is highly unorthodox. I'm not prepared for a sentencing hearing."

"And Mr. Bean, it is also highly unorthodox for lawyers to tell me how to do my job in my own court. The city wants two weeks' jail time, a thousand-dollar fine, and six months' probation, right?"

Mr. Bean looked perplexed. "Well, yes."

Judge Thurmond nodded. "And I assume Ms. Clark intends to pursue a civil matter in this court to pay for emotional trauma and any plastic surgery she will need. Mr. Bean, would you mind leaning over the rail and asking Ms. Clark if she does intend to sue Ms. Walker?"

"Are you serious?" asked Mr. Bean.

"Young man, I once threw my gavel at a young lawyer who asked me too many questions. They needed the jaws of life to extract my gavel from his skull."

The life drained from Mr. Bean's face. He covered his head with one hand while he spun around and began talking to Gemima.

After a moment he turned back around. "Ms. Clark does intend to pursue the civil matter."

"Super," said Judge Thurmond. "We'll just handle that matter now."

"Your Honor, I'm the city's lawyer. I don't represent Ms. Clark."

"You do now."

"That's… that's not how things work, Your Honor."

Judge Thurmond turned to the side and started talking to no one in particular. "There he goes again, asking me a bunch of questions." He tossed his gavel into the air and caught it after one rotation. "I wonder if I still have the magic." He leaned over and spoke to the court reporter. "Be ready to call 911 in case my gavel gets stuck again."

Mr. Bean looked around the court like he didn't know what to do. I'm pretty sure he thought Judge Thurmond was crazy. And I'm certain *I* thought the judge was crazy.

Judge Thurmond pointed at Mr. Bean with his left hand as he started to go through a throwing motion with his right arm. I really wanted to see how hard the judge could throw that gavel.

But Mr. Bean spoke quickly. "I—I guess I could represent her if you really want me to."

Judge Thurmond stopped and smiled. "See, that wasn't so hard. Okay, I'm the judge, so I can do pretty much whatever I want. And I don't want to ever have to deal with this case ever again, so I'm going to proceed to the civil action now."

"Now?" Mr. Bean squeaked.

Judge Thurmond narrowed his eyes at the city lawyer. "Yes, Mr. Bean. *Now.* But don't worry, this should be simple enough. Ms. Walker admits to what she did, so let's just throw that judgment in now. How much would Ms. Clark like for emotional damage?"

I started to panic. I didn't want to go to jail. And I didn't have any money. I had thought Judge Thurmond might go easy on me. Now I was worried.

Mr. Bean looked at the judge uncertainly, then turned around and whispered with Gemima. After a moment he turned back around. "Ms. Clark believes another thousand dollars for emotional damage would be fair."

"And how much for the plastic surgery? I hear that can get expensive."

The lawyer and Gemima conferred for a minute on this one. Then finally, "Ten thousand, Your Honor."

"Sure you don't want more?"

"Twenty?"

"That sounds better," said Judge Thurmond.

Now I was freaking out. My body was shaking. My chest was thump, thump, thumping away.

"Okay," said the judge, "let's wrap this up. Ms. Walker, I take it you realize the serious nature of what you have done."

I was furious at myself for being so stupid. Stupid in punching Gemima. Stupid *and stubborn* in refusing to get a lawyer. But at this point, there wasn't much I could do.

"I do, Your Honor."

"I'm glad to hear it. In considering the legal and the civil matters together, I sentence you, Hope Walker, to the following."

He cleared his throat.

"You will serve zero days in jail. You will pay the city zero dollars in fines. You will pay Ms. Clark zero dollars for emotional trauma. As for plastic surgery, you will buy her exactly one New York strip from Randy the butcher. Those run about $8.99."

I couldn't believe it. And judging by the outburst from Gemima and Mr. Bean, they couldn't either.

Judge Thurmond banged his gavel to regain order.

Mr. Bean, who looked like he was physically restraining Gemima from leaping from her seat, stood. "A steak, Your Honor?"

Judge Thurmond smiled. "I saw it on *Leave It to Beaver*. They put a steak on the Beaver's black eye. Apparently it makes it better. I suggest Ms. Clark do that."

"Your Honor, I have to strenuously object," said Mr. Bean.

The judge spoke to the court reporter. "Gladys, be sure you got that correct. Mr. Bean strenuously objects."

"Got it, Your Honor. Strenuously."

"Your Honor!" Mr. Bean's face was turning red. "This is a *serious* offense, and you are making a mockery of not only the law, but now, of, um… my client! May I at least ask why?"

"First of all, Mr. Bean, I couldn't give two craps about how you think things should be done. I have been a judge for over thirty years and have devoted my life to the law. The only mockery here is Ms. Clark claiming that she is some kind of *victim*. You see, I received a call earlier today from an old and very dear friend. He told me several stories about what Ms. Clark did to his child during high school. Those stories made me sick to my stomach. I've heard from three more people since that call. All with similar stories. Had any one of these incidents been brought to my courtroom, I would have gladly thrown the book at Ms. Clark."

"Your Honor, none of that has *any* bearing on today's proceedings!"

"Thank you, Mr. Bean, for once again telling me how to do my job. If you do it again, I will find you in contempt of court, and you will spend the next twenty-four hours in a cell thinking about how to speak to me in my courtroom. Now—there's an old legal term that I believe is quite relevant to this matter today. I don't remember the Latin, but the English is plain enough. *She had it coming to her.*" He grabbed his gavel and raised it, but then paused. "Before I bring this matter to a close, I have one more request. Sheriff Kramer, could you do me a favor?"

"Yes, Your Honor."

"Please do not waste my time again."

Judge Thurmond banged his gavel, and court was adjourned.

~ ⚭ ~

I pulled a ten-dollar bill out of my wallet, crumpled it up, walked over to Gemima, and threw it at her. "Keep the change."

She ripped off her sunglasses and screamed. Mr. Bean had to hold her back.

Katie gave me a big hug at the back of the courtroom. "That was the greatest takedown of Gemima I have ever seen in my life," she said.

"Judge Thurmond is officially my favorite person in the world right now." And Dr. Bridges. I would have to remember to thank him. And, apparently, three other people, if I could just find out who.

I turned to Granny. "Did you call him today?"

"Nope."

"You sure?"

She crossed her heart. "Promise. But I can tell you this: he'll be drinking for free for a while. That was glorious."

I felt a tap on my shoulder and turned around. It was Alex.

"You got a minute to talk, Hope?"

He had been given a minor dressing-down by Judge Thurmond, and he didn't look too happy about it. Not a hint of a smile. Not handsome Alex at the moment.

I turned to Katie and Granny, and they got the picture. "We'll be outside if you need us," Katie said.

They walked away, and Alex and I stepped alone into the marble hallway outside of Judge Thurmond's courtroom.

"Listen, Hope… I'm glad the judge didn't punish you."

"Fine, can I go?"

He held his hands up, palms out. "But you must understand, I had a job to do."

"Thanks for the reminder, can I go?"

"Stop it, Hope. Just—"

"Just what? Do whatever it is you want me to do? Sorry, kiddo, that's not who I am."

"Why are you so angry with me? I was just doing my job."

I folded my arms. "Are you really that dumb?"

"What did you expect me to do?"

"For starters? When I step out of a bathroom, how about I don't have to see you kissing Gemima Clark?"

"*She* kissed *me*, Hope!"

"So all of a sudden Big Sheriff Alex Kramer can't fend off a girl? Is that what you're saying?"

"That's not what I'm saying. She kissed me, then it was over and you punched her. Why'd you have to punch her?"

"Did you not just listen to Judge Thurmond in there? I punched Gemima because she is horrible and has always *been* horrible. I punched her for all the times I *didn't* punch her in the past. And yes, I punched her because she was kissing you!"

Alex growled. "She said she wanted to press charges. I had to arrest you."

"No, Alex, that's where you're wrong. You did not. If you had any guts, you would have stood up to her. You would have said no, you jumped on top of me and started kissing me without me asking, and this girl I... this girl I was with saw it and she got mad and punched you because you deserve it and everybody knows it and I'm not going to arrest her. That's what you should have done!" I shouted that last part. The sound echoed in the hall.

Alex stepped back as if to regroup. He looked like he was about to say something, then caught himself, shook his head, and took a breath.

"Listen, Hope, right before court started, I got a call from Debbie and Cal Ruttledge. They told me there was another animal shooting. And that you were there. They said you chased the shooter into the woods. Hope, you could have been hurt."

"But I wasn't."

"You were right about the goat case. I gave that to you because I was messing with you. But this is two shootings now. Someone's doing this intentionally. And you can't just go running after people like that."

"Why?"

"Because you might get hurt!"

"And why would that matter to you?"

"You… you are so infuriating. Isn't it obvious?"

"You arrested me last night, so no, whatever you think is obvious… is definitely not obvious."

Alex put his hands on his hips. "What do you want me to do?"

"How about you say you're sorry?"

"Fine. I'm sorry."

"Okay, now answer my question. Have you ever been in a serious relationship?"

"Yes."

"Now why was that so hard?"

He said nothing.

"You know why? It's because you don't trust me."

That caught him off guard. "What are you talking about?"

"I'm talking about the murder weapon."

He looked confused. "What?"

"Imagine my surprise this morning when Dr. Bridges told me that the murder weapon was a screwdriver. A flathead screwdriver. Not a knife."

His eyes widened with understanding. No more confusion. He took another step back.

"Alex, you told me it was a knife. Why did you tell me it was a knife?"

He still said nothing. He didn't need to.

"I already know why," I said. "Because you knew from the beginning, just like me, that this case was going to be almost impossible to solve. Except that... we have this one thing. This one piece of evidence. The murder weapon. And apart from you, Dr. Bridges, and now me, the only person who knows what the murder weapon was... is the murderer. That's important. You want to keep that secret. And that's why you didn't tell me. Because you didn't want that little fact getting out."

The look on his face told me everything I needed to know.

"In other words, Alex Kramer, you don't trust me."

∿ CHAPTER TWENTY-ONE ∿

I went back to the Library, climbed the stairs to my apartment, and collapsed into my bed. I dreamt about a monstrous skeletal arm that was wreaking havoc through the streets of Tokyo… except it wasn't really Tokyo, it was Main Street in Hopeless. Anyway, there was a family trapped in a car, and the monster hand was coming down to crush them. And one of the kids had a straw in his mouth and was shooting spitwads at the creature, and that made the creature angry. So of course I throw myself in harm's way like the classic heroine I am.

Except, at the very last minute, Sheriff Alex Kramer comes along. It doesn't look like Alex—it looks like a combination of Sheriff Ed Kline and Mr. Clowder—but in the dream I know it's Alex because, well, he's still got those green eyes. And I think he's here to save me—and the family!

But instead, he walks up to me, and he says…

"Hope Walker, you have the right to remain silent."

That's when my face buzzed.

A moment later my face buzzed again, and I realized I

was sleeping on my phone. I lifted up my head, and actual slobber fell from my lip.

Oh, that's just lovely.

I saw that it was Katie, so I hit the green button.

"Hope, it's Katie."

"I know it's Katie. It says Katie on my phone when your number rings. It's part of the technical magic behind these new things called cell phones."

"Okay, Miss Grumpy Shorts. I can tell I woke you."

"For your information, I've been out working."

"Liar. I can hear the drool through the phone."

How does she do that?

"I changed my mind about tonight. After the day you had, coming over to say goodnight to my children is the last thing you need to do."

"You sure they won't be mad?"

"Are you kidding? I promised they could watch *Die Hard* as their bedtime movie."

"I think the hero murders about a hundred people in that one."

I could almost hear her shrug. "Yippee ki yay."

"Katie—I think this is the part where I criticize your parenting technique, and then you criticize me for being a know-it-all single person who doesn't actually have any kids…"

"Hope, what I'm saying is, tonight, you need a ladies' night."

That woke me up a little. "That's actually a very good idea. One problem: I don't want to show my face at the Taco House for a while."

"Are you kidding me? You're the girl who punched Gemima Clark! You're like a national treasure. If anything, you'll have to worry about signing autographs."

"I'm not really in the mood to sign autographs tonight. How about we just get a case of Bud and go down to the river?"

"I can see you're in a very bad place."

"What? It *is* the King of Beers."

"Snap out of it, Hope. Me and you. Girls' night. Alcohol. Unhealthy food. We talk about people behind their backs. It'll make us feel better about ourselves. Come on!"

I sat up and wiped the remaining slobber off my phone. "I do have one idea. What are your feelings on apple donuts?"

Thankfully, Miss "No Ifs, Ands, or Buts" was not at the ticket counter, and the younger girl who was there was a lot more agreeable. When I claimed we were there on official business—Katie even showed her an ID badge she had from working at the sheriff's office—she let us in.

When we passed through the haystack tunnel and the first food smells started to wash over us, I thought Katie was going to cry. She turned and gave me a hug.

"I'm someplace fun—and I'm here without children… which makes it *actually* fun. It's been so, so long."

"I *actually* had fun with your kids when we were here on Saturday."

"That's because you were just swooping in. Swooping in

is always fun. It's all the other stuff that's not fun."

"But isn't it all the other stuff that's supposed to make you a better person?"

She pointed to her face. "Do I look like a better person to you?"

"You really don't."

"Yeah, I didn't think so."

We stopped at Popeye's Pints to grab a couple mugs of beer, then we made a beeline down Apple Donut Lane to the main attraction.

"Oh, hoochie mama," Katie said when the attendant piled a half dozen warm donuts into a paper basket.

"Now remember," I said as I reached for my first donut, "three of these are mine."

She slapped my hand away. "Like hell they are."

"Katie, step away from the donuts and no one will get hurt."

Katie pointed to a sign behind the clerk. "But they are America's *Best* Donuts. A woman of my appetite cannot just have three of America's Best Donuts."

"I promise we'll get more later. We need to pace ourselves."

"You really don't understand the concept of Ladies' Night, do you?"

Lucinda popped out from her kitchen carrying four boxes of donuts, but when she saw me, she set them down and walked over.

"Business or pleasure tonight, Hope?"

"A little bit of both," I said. "Lucinda Meadows, this is

my friend Katie Rodgers."

Lucinda stuck out her hand, and Katie shook it.

"Rodgers," Lucinda said. "Wasn't it your son who found Wanda's arm in the pumpkin patch on Saturday?"

Katie smiled. "It was a really proud moment for all of us. We've been looking for dead bodies in pumpkin patches for years. And to think… we finally did it."

Lucinda looked at her like she was crazy. Then she turned to me with a questioning look.

"Yes," I said. "She's kidding."

"Good. So… how's the investigation coming?"

"It really just started."

"Any leads?"

"Honestly? Not really."

Katie lifted her finger while she swallowed a big hunk of donut. "I object."

"Excuse me?" I said.

"I think the culprit was…" She slowly pointed at Lucinda. "You." Then she broke out into a big smile. "Because girl, you are *killing* me with these donuts."

Lucinda and I both laughed.

"In fact," Katie continued, "they are almost so good that I don't want to drink my beer." On cue, she took a big swig of beer and wiped her lips with the back of her hand. "I said *almost*. Seriously, Lucinda. I don't even understand how an apple donut can be this good."

I leaned toward her. "You know what the secret ingredient is, don't you?"

Katie leaned in as well.

"Love!" I said, and proceeded to give her a big kiss on the cheek.

"Gross!" Katie yelped. "Not cool, Hope Walker. And just for that, I'm taking one of your donuts." She grabbed a fourth donut and popped it into her mouth before I could stop her.

"How about you, Lucinda?" I asked. "Any more thoughts on what might have happened?"

"Plenty of *thoughts*. I mean, everyone is still talking about it. But no one knows anything. I don't think anybody around here could have done it… but…"

"But what?"

"Have you talked to Johnny yet?"

"Just talked to him this morning. Why?"

"It was something Mary said to me during lunch today. About Johnny being creepy."

"He is creepy. Super creepy. And I know that from only ten minutes spent at his home. This is a surprise to you?"

"I guess that's just it. I've known him so long I got used to it. I thought of Johnny as eccentric. But Mary reminded me how creepy everybody thought he was when he first started working here."

"You think he's creepy enough to have killed an old woman and buried her in a pumpkin patch?"

She hesitated, then picked up her boxes of donuts. "Maybe."

And then she walked away.

After finishing our donuts and beer, I asked Katie if she wanted to walk around for a while. She patted her belly and burped. "No, I definitely do not want to walk around for a while."

I spotted the train station, and had another idea. "Think you can make it as far as that train?"

"Sure… but only if you roll me."

The train was driven by an old man who announced himself as "Boom Boom." He said he drove the train part-time as a way to get away from his wife. Then he laughed. And that made all the men on the train laugh as well. I didn't see the women laughing very much.

The train snaked its way through the park, and it really was incredible to see how large Bubba's had grown. I thought back to my conversation with Mary; it was really hard to imagine that this place had ever struggled. But I remembered enough about it to know that the smaller and gentler pumpkin patch I knew in my youth probably *had* struggled. Most businesses failed, after all. And Bubba's was a weird kind of business.

Among other amusements, we passed by a zombie-themed go-cart raceway, what might be the world's largest bouncy house, a "slime house" that I was thankful Dominic never found, and a gigantic brown-and-yellow barn that, fascinatingly enough, sold nothing but cake. Katie almost launched herself out of the train when she saw a triple fudge cake through a window. We passed Wanda's World and saw not only her old dragon but the other fantastic beasts she had created. We passed Johnny's World and witnessed a fairly impressive laser light show while a robot danced to the beat of Michael Jackson's "Beat it."

And then we approached a second train station, the one that marked the halfway point of our ride, I noticed what stood right next to it.

My old nemesis.

The corn maze.

Katie saw it too. Her eyes lit up, and she punched me in the shoulder. "Hope! It's the haunted corn maze! We should totally do it."

I stepped off the train and looked at it warily.

"Not a chance."

Katie came up alongside me. "You're still not afraid of it, are you? We were little kids back then. We are full-grown adults now."

"Exactly. I'm an adult, which means I don't have to prove myself to anybody."

"You don't really think that's what it means to be an adult, do you?"

"You got a better definition?"

"I've got ten better definitions."

"Name one."

"Being an adult means doing crap you hate every day and acting like you enjoy it."

"We're talking about your kids again, aren't we?"

"Hope, you were a little kid when you got lost in there. You can't avoid stuff like this forever. When you do, it doesn't make you happy."

"And now we're talking about me being gone from Hopeless so long."

Katie spread her arms. "Of course we are. All I'm saying is, you are a brave, intelligent, and strong woman. If you've got any cobwebs left in that thick skull of yours, you need to face them—clear them out."

I looked at the haunted corn maze. If possible, it was even bigger and more terrifying than it was when I was a child. Then I saw a green tractor coming our way, with Kip Granger behind the wheel. He was returning with a group of hayrack riders.

Katie smiled. "So, you gonna do the corn maze?"

"Someday, I promise."

"But?"

I started toward Farmer Granger. "But first, I need to solve a murder."

~ CHAPTER TWENTY-TWO ~

Kip handed the tractor over to a young farmhand, then unscrewed the cap from an old thermos and took a swig of whatever was in there.

"Mr. Granger?"

He looked at me sideways. "Mr. Granger was my dad. The name's Kip."

"Hi, Kip, my name is Hope Walker, and this is my friend Katie."

Kip looked at us like he could not possibly care less. "You need something?"

"I want to talk to you about the death of Wanda Wegman."

His face soured. "Not interested." He screwed the lid back onto his thermos and began to walk away.

I caught up to him immediately. "I'm working with Sheriff Kramer. I think he told you I might be stopping by."

"He did. Still not interested."

"Why?"

"Because she's dead, and there's nothing any of us can do about it."

"But she was murdered!"

"Which is tragic. Still nothing I can do about it."

"Kip! Don't you know what people are saying?"

He stopped and narrowed his eyes at me. "What are people saying?"

"They're saying you did it."

He seemed to consider what I'd said. The gravity of it. Then he spit something thick and brown onto the dirt between his feet. "I didn't hurt Wanda."

"People are saying that since her body was found in your pumpkin patch, you're probably the one who put her there."

He pulled out a pocket knife and started digging dirt from under his fingernails. "That's just stupid."

"Stupid or not, it's what people are saying. You know what else they're saying? They're saying, how could that body be in his patch for three years and he never once finds it?"

"I didn't hurt Wanda."

"I believe you. But other people don't. They think you're an old crusty farmer who had a motive to kill her."

"What are you talking about?"

"People know, Kip."

He folded up his pocket knife. "Know what?"

"That you loved Wanda… and once upon a time, she broke your heart."

That got his attention. He walked over to a picnic table, sat down, took off his green cap, and squeezed it between his strong, calloused hands. "People know about me and Wanda?"

I sat down with him, Katie beside me. "Yep."

He shrugged. "I don't know if it was love. I don't know if I've ever really *loved* anyone. But... it was probably the closest a guy like me will ever come."

"And she broke it off?"

He nodded.

"Why?"

He shrugged. "The usual reason, I guess. She didn't like me as much as I liked her."

"Did she tell you that?"

He laughed as if he was remembering something. "She actually did. Wanda was like that. Honest. To a fault."

"Plenty of people have told me she was hard to get along with."

"For sure. Partly because of her honesty. She believed your yes should mean yes and your no should mean no. That got her into lots of trouble with people. It's also what I loved about her."

"So... after she broke it off?"

"Nothing. We still interacted at work, just like always. It was probably weirder for me than it was for her. She didn't get all tied up in knots with her emotions."

"But she did get angry about stuff. I've heard about her arguments."

"Oh, she got into plenty of arguments all right. She was a smart woman, and she thought she was always right. She usually was, which only bothered people even more."

"So, Kip... the story that's forming around here is that you dated, she broke it off, you got mad at her, and you killed her."

"That's a funny way of showing you like someone, ain't it?"

"It is. It's also the kind of thing that people believe."

"Why are you even here, Miss Walker? You're a reporter. If that's the story you're fixin' to write, I can't stop you."

"The only story I intend to write is the truth."

"Then what is it that you want, exactly?"

"Information. Do you have any insight—anything, big or small—that might help explain who did this and why?"

He stood up and ran his hands through his hair. Then he put his hat back on his head. "I have an idea… but it doesn't make any sense to me. Wanda got into a big, big argument right before she went missing. And now that she's dead, I can't help but wonder if it's connected."

"A big argument?" That sounded like just the lead we needed. "Did you tell Sheriff Kramer about it?"

"Well, no."

"Why not?"

"I didn't think anybody around here was capable of hurting her. I still don't think that."

"Then what's changed? Why are you telling me now?"

"Because now I've apparently become a suspect."

"Who was Wanda arguing with, Kip?"

He looked around like he wanted to make sure nobody was watching us. Then he leaned in and lowered his voice. "She was arguing with Mary. I don't know what it was about, but whatever it was, Wanda was mad. She was really, *really* mad."

~∞~

I wanted to talk to Bubba about this argument his wife had with the deceased. Kip said we'd find Bubba down at the pumpkin catapult—and Katie saw that as a sign we should get snow cones.

I didn't understand the logic in that—I doubted there *was* any logic in that—but I was all in. So we each got a mongo-sized snow cone at the Spooky Shaved Ice Shop, and that instantly made me feel like a ten-year-old girl again.

"Hard to imagine Mary Riley killing someone isn't it?" I said. "She seems so nice."

"You should know by now that appearances can be deceiving," said Katie. Her tongue was already turning blue from the dye.

"Of course, it's possible that Kip is just making this up in order to deflect attention from himself."

"I'd say that's a very strong possibility."

There was a long pause while I dealt with a big chunk of ice that wanted to fall off the side of my cone. Katie apparently took this as some kind of opening.

"So... where do you and Alex go from here?"

"There is no 'me and Alex.'"

"Okay, maybe not at this precise moment... but it doesn't have to stay that way."

I looked at her sideways. "Yes, I think it does."

Katie rubbed her fingers into her temples like she was having a migraine. "You really can be very irritating sometimes."

"What's that supposed to mean?"

"It means you would be a very bad married person."

"I agree. Still offended though," I said.

"Good. Hope, I love you. You know I do."

"Can we leave it at that before you say 'but'?"

"No, honey, we can't. Because this is a big but. And as someone with a *very* big butt, I'm an authority on that subject. So listen up."

I rolled my eyes.

Katie pointed a finger at me. "Don't you dare roll your eyes at me, young lady. Now here's the deal. You would be a bad married person because marriage is hard. Married people get stressed and impatient and mad at each other all the time. And then they forgive each other and try to get a little better... and then they move on."

"Your point?"

"My point is you like him, Hope. I can see it. Everyone can see it."

"Everyone?"

She nodded. "Everyone."

"That's... embarrassing."

"Why?"

I froze.

Katie nodded. "Ah. I see. Everyone knows you like him, and that's embarrassing to you because, when something bad happens—and you always assume it will—then it will be that much harder for you to brush it off like it wasn't real. Because everybody knows."

That punch landed squarely.

"Listen up, buttercup. You like him. And trust me, he likes you."

"You really think so?"

"He *likes* you, Hope. And the two of you were *on a date*. You weren't comparing notes on an investigation. It was a date. And it was going great, until Lady Horrible showed up. And then she did a bad thing and you reacted badly, and Alex reacted badly to you reacting badly. Do you know how much crap like that there is in marriage?"

"How much?"

"Hope, that *is* marriage!"

"Does it get better?"

"Of course it does. If you try."

"Do you and Chris try?"

"Not every day. But on the whole, yes. I know I make a lot of jokes... but I am a better person today than I was five years ago."

I laughed. "You must have really sucked five years ago."

"You're a butthead, Hope."

"But I'm *your* butthead, Katie."

"The truth is, I react badly less often than I used to. And he reacts badly to my reacting badly less often, too. It still happens, and it will always happen. But each of us is less selfish than we used to be. And we're more patient than we used to be."

"And you're much hotter than you used to be."

Katie posed like she was a model. "It's the mommy boobs and the hair that won't curl anymore and the bags under my eyes. It's the perfect combination!"

"So what are you saying, oh wise one?"

Katie wrapped her free arm around my shoulder and

squeezed. "Get over your stupid prideful self and take a chance. And in the process… give Alex another chance."

We had arrived at the catapult, where a large pumpkin was just landing on the front hood of the old pickup truck two hundred feet away. The kids went nuts.

"Remember," Bubba roared as the crowd dispersed, "the next launching of the catapult is in exactly thirty minutes!"

Katie and I caught up to Bubba before he could move on to whatever he had to do next. He smiled when he saw me and shook my hand firmly—looking me straight in the eye and patting my shoulder. Bubba Riley was an expert hand-shaker.

"Mr. Riley, you remember me? Hope Walker. And this is my friend Katie."

"Of course I remember you. Call me Bubba." He gave Katie the same warm greeting, then turned back to me. "I take it you want to talk?"

"If you could spare a minute."

He shrugged. "I really can't. Busy night at the patch. But if you can keep up with me, I'd be glad to chat." He took off walking without waiting for a reply.

Katie lagged behind, but I managed to match his pace.

"So," he said. "Any headway on the investigation?"

"Nothing firm. Just talking to people. Getting a picture of Wanda. Who she was, what made her tick, relationships. That kind of thing."

"No leads then?"

"I'm afraid not."

"Well, how can I help?"

"You told the sheriff that Wanda was hard to get along with. Seems like everyone else agrees. She liked to be right, wasn't shy about telling people they were wrong, and that led to a lot of arguments. Is all that fair?"

"Yeah, that's spot on. She told it like it was."

"Did anything else about Wanda lead to arguments?"

Bubba gave me a blank look.

"Was she mean?"

Bubba considered that. "She was stubborn and prideful… and some thought that was rude. But she wasn't *mean*, so to speak."

"Was she petty or vindictive?" I asked.

"Nope and nope. Like I said, she was honest." He made a face. "Let me put it like this. Me and my buddies Earl and Buddy Ray have a regular golfing date. I can't make it during the season, but otherwise, every Monday evening, nine holes of golf. You know what a mulligan is?"

"It's when you get an extra shot."

"Yeah, you mess up, you hit the shot again. It's a mulligan. The boys and I give each other one mulligan a round. And you can buy an extra one if you give each guy two bucks."

"What's this have to do with Wanda?"

"Wanda Wegman wouldn't take a mulligan in a million years. And if she knew that's how the boys and me played, she'd give me the business about it. Like I said—she was honest." We arrived in front of Wanda's World, and he looked impatient. "Sorry, I'm in a bit of a time crunch—I have to go inside and run the dragon."

"Time to smash a pumpkin?"

"After all these years, it's still a highlight. Was there anything else you needed?"

"One thing. On Saturday, you mentioned that you and Wanda got into arguments from time to time—that you didn't always see eye to eye about how to run things around here. You and Mary both said that Wanda's run off before, so you assumed she got angry about something this time and ran off again."

"Yes, that's right."

"The thing is, that doesn't sound like the whole story. I mean, it doesn't really make sense that you thought Wanda ran off because she was just mad in general. It makes more sense that you believed she ran off because you already knew she was mad about something in particular. That you knew of something specific that had set her off."

"What are you trying to say?"

"What I'm trying to say is, I heard that just before she disappeared, Wanda got into a particular argument with someone here. A *big* argument. One that made Wanda very, *very* angry."

"With who?"

"With your wife. With Mary."

Bubba stepped back, and his eyes widened. "That's not true."

"I heard it from a very reliable source."

"It didn't happen."

"How can you be so certain?"

"Because… because Mary's not the one who got into an argument with Wanda. It was me."

Now I was the one to look surprised. "Wanda was mad at you?"

"Yes."

"What was the fight about?"

He rubbed his hand across his face. "It was stupid. Wanda thought the next big exhibit at the patch should be a barn where kids could go and shoot plastic balls at each other. I disagreed. I wanted a big indoor food cafeteria for when it rained. I told her my decision was final, and she was madder than a hornet. But Hope, I didn't kill her. I couldn't. Wanda was like family to me."

"That might be true, Bubba, but if you really got into a big fight with her... *right* before she was murdered... then that makes you the prime suspect."

"That's ridiculous."

"That's how it's going to look." I wanted to give Bubba a chance to change his story. "You sure it was you who had the fight with Wanda?"

Bubba hesitated. His forehead bunched up. I couldn't tell what was going on inside his head, but I could tell *something* was going on. Was he trying to think up a lie? Kip had no reason to lie about Wanda's fight with Mary, but it was possible he was mistaken. It was also possible that Bubba was simply covering for his wife.

His face shifted. The forehead wrinkles disappeared as he relaxed into his normal easygoing smile. "Afraid I'm out of time for tonight. Wanda may not be here any longer, but her dragon is—and the show must go on. Pardon me, Hope Walker, I've got a pumpkin to smash."

Katie caught up to me as Bubba walked away.

"Figure anything out?"

"Maybe," I said.

"I see that gleam in your eye. You've got an idea."

"The possibility of an idea."

"Care to share?"

"Not just yet."

"You about ready to go?"

"Yeah, I actually am. My feet are killing me and I'm tired," I said.

"Me too. But there's one thing we have to do first."

"Please don't say the corn maze."

"Good guess. Nope, something much more important."

"What?"

Katie smiled. "We need to grab more donuts."

～o CHAPTER TWENTY-THREE o～

I was in the bathroom the next morning—and watching videos of goats stumbling down playground slides—when my phone buzzed with a text message.

Hot chick is here

My brain and belly were both suffering from a not-insignificant apple donut hangover, so it took me a second for the message to register.

Is this Nick?

OC

What does OC mean?

Of course… old lady

Are you sure it's her?

She's the only hot chick in this town

He had insulted me twice, but I didn't care. I was on a mission.

Can you keep her there long enough for me to get there?

Easy

You sure?

Yep. Hot chick wants to meet you.

When I walked into A Hopeless Cup ten minutes later, Nick and Madeline were busy behind the counter, and there was only one customer in the coffee shop.

The woman from the picture.

Ms. Jones.

She had on gray tights and a pink jogging quarter-zip, and she sat at a table, one leg crossed over the other, her back straight and perfect, sipping her coffee.

There was another coffee across from her.

She did not look my way.

I walked to the table and looked at the untouched cup of coffee. "White Mocha Latte" was written in Sharpie on the side.

I gestured to the empty chair.

Finally, Ms. Jones looked up at me. And she was indeed beautiful. She had the high cheekbones of a model and almost flawless skin. Her hair was a brilliant blonde, with just a few light brown highlights. But her lips were thin and cruel. And her eyes… I now understood what Mr. Clowder had meant. They were a cold, soulless gray.

She took another sip of her coffee. "The barista said you drink white mocha latte."

"Thank you," I said as I grabbed my coffee and sat.

She smelled of coconut oil. And some other aroma I couldn't quite place.

"So, Ms. Walker," she said.

I took a sip of my coffee. Perfect as usual. "Ms. Jones, I presume."

She nodded.

"I understand you wanted to meet," I said.

"I understand you've been showing my picture around town."

"You came up in an investigation of mine."

She squinted. "I heard something about a goat being shot?"

"Murdered is more like it."

"Didn't know goats could be murdered."

"They can. So can cows."

"This is thrilling. But what does any of it have to do with me?"

"I heard you've been visiting the people on Moose Mountain, trying to convince them to sell their cabins."

"Yes. I'm an independent real estate broker and I have an investor who's interested in the properties."

"Who is this investor?"

"The kind of person who prefers to remain anonymous in the early part of a project."

"What kind of 'project'?"

"The kind of project that I don't talk about, so I can do a good job getting the best value for my client."

"And have you?"

"Have I what?"

"Done a good job?"

She blinked several times. "Sadly, I have not. Try as I might, the people of Hopeless have not responded to my charms."

"I hear Wilma Jenkins is having some luck."

"I wouldn't know. But it's always nice to see a strong woman do well for herself."

"Do you own a gun?" I asked.

She tapped her fingernails against the table. "I own several."

"And did you fire one of these guns at Percy?"

"Who's Percy?"

"The goat. The goat you killed."

"That's quite an accusation."

"You didn't deny it."

Her tongue danced across her thin, cruel lips. Then she cocked her head. "I deny it now. Categorically. I am a law-abiding citizen of the United States of America. I don't shoot animals. I don't speed. I don't jaywalk. I don't even litter. I am a businesswoman, Ms. Walker. That's why I wanted to meet you. To make that clear to you."

"So the rest is just some big coincidence?"

"The rest? You mean the goat? You want to know if it is a coincidence that a goat got shot in the same town where I happen to be working as a real estate broker? The very question is bizarre, Ms. Walker. But you're an investigator, so I want you to have the facts. And the facts here are clear.

"First, whoever this alleged 'goat murderer' is, it's not me. And second, I don't like it when people accuse me of things I didn't do. And… hypothetically… if someone were to ever do that—you know, accuse me of something? I would take that kind of thing personally." She stood. "Very personally."

She looked at me with those cold, soulless eyes, and then she tipped her head forward just a bit. "Ms. Walker." And she walked away, tossed her empty cup in the trash, and left.

A shiver ran down my spine. Ms. Jones was serious, grade-A villain, straight out of central casting for a Bond movie.

I suddenly wondered what kind of car she drove. I ran outside to see a car reversing out of its parking place, with Ms. Jones in the driver's seat. But it wasn't red, and it wasn't a sedan. It was a black SUV. Not that this surprised me. If she was behind the animal shootings, she wouldn't have used her own car. She was too smart for that.

But then I thought of something.

Maybe she wasn't *always* smart.

I went back in, grabbed a napkin, and carefully used it to remove her paper coffee cup from the trash can. Then I took out my phone and called Darwin.

Darwin worked in IT for my old paper, the *Portland News Gazette*. But on the side, he was the best researcher I'd ever met. And a pretty fair hacker. *And* I had leverage.

He'd had a crush on me for as long as I'd known him.

"Hope, I'm in the middle of something right now."

"What?"

"Sleep. It's six forty-five in the morning. I'm in the middle of sleep."

"You do realize that one day, when we share a house together, I'm not going to cotton to that attitude of yours, mister."

"Did you just say cotton to?"

"It's an old person's saying. And since we're going to be growing old together…"

"Can we go back to the times when you just joked about us going on a date sometime?"

"Darwin, you know that I only have eyes for you."

"I categorically do not know that."

"Well, you should… after all we've been through the last few months."

"I haven't even seen you in a few months."

"But this thing you and I've got."

"Which is only over the phone."

"Exactly! This thing we have over the phone is so perfect, I don't know how you could have any doubts about us anymore."

"Can you just ask me for the favor? I really am tired."

"I'm sending you a package. In that package is a coffee cup. I need you to find fingerprints, DNA, the works. Tell me whatever you can about the person who used that cup."

"Hope, I'm not a forensic scientist."

I laughed. "Come on, my snuggle bunny. I know you're not a forensic scientist. I also know you can do almost *anything*."

"That is technically true."

"Of course it is."

"Hope?"

"Yes, Darwin."

"I thought we talked about 'snuggle bunny.'"

My next stop was the *Hopeless News*, where my boss, Earl Denton, was busy whacking away at the antique printing press with a Louisville slugger.

"Doing some fine-tuning, Earl?"

Earl let loose a torrent of near-obscenities, a language almost entirely his own, made up of words that weren't obscene but sounded like maybe they should be. Then he smashed the printing press one last time and stepped back, looking at the machine as if maybe he'd just dealt the death blow.

Miraculously, the printing press roared to life. Earl raised both arms in triumph and walked right past me like some conquering hero. He reached under his desk, pulled out a bottle of Jim Beam, and took a swig.

"Earl, isn't it seven in the morning a little early even for you?"

"You haven't seen the things I've seen."

"We're talking about an old printing press, not a firefight in the Mekong Delta."

Earl sat down and kicked his feet up on his desk. "Update me on this murder investigation."

"Which one?"

Earl arched an eyebrow. "There's more than one?"

"You haven't heard about Mr. Clowder's goat, Percy?"

"Percy's dead?"

"Shot in broad daylight."

Earl raised his glass in solemn fashion. "To one of the best wethers I've ever seen."

"You know what a wether is?" I asked.

"Who doesn't? And why didn't you tell me about Percy?"

"I've been busy with the other murder investigation."

He raised a finger off of his glass. "That one I did hear about. And we'll get to that. But what happened to Percy?"

I told him everything—about Percy, the note, the Rutledges' cow. And I told him what I thought was going on with Mayor Jenkins and the cabins, using Ms. Jones to scaring people into selling their land. And I finished up with the strange Bond-villain coffee shop meeting.

"So," he said, "a little *mano a mano*?"

"Like Al Pacino and Robert De Niro finally facing off in the movie *Heat*."

"Which one are you?"

"I think I'm Al Pacino."

Earl poured himself another glass of whiskey and took a nice long sip. Then he shook his head. "That is one whale of a story." He leaned over his desk and stabbed his long bony finger at me. "But Hope, we've got to be right about this one. You've got to do the work. Really do the work. This Ms. Jones? She's a brazen one. And that probably means she's smart."

"You're thinking it's going to be difficult to prove a connection between her and Wilma?"

"I'm thinking it's going to be difficult to prove a lot of things. In my experience, when a great deal of money is at stake, people, bad people, work really hard to get that money. And they don't' much care for nosy reporters who get in their way. Work the problem, Hope. Work the story. And then, when you've got it… when you've really got it…" He trailed off, his fingers tap-tap-tapping away at this desk.

"What?" I asked.

He leaned over the desk again, his eyes full of intensity. "We nail Wilma Jenkins to the wall." He took another sip of his whiskey. "Now, tell me about Wanda Wegman."

And so I did. I told him about Dominic finding the skeleton arm. He howled at that. I told him about finding out it was Wanda. About Dr. Bridges finding the murder weapon. About Alex withholding that piece of evidence from me. And about all the conversations I'd had with the employees at Bubba's Pumpkin Patch.

"So, any ideas?" I asked when I had finished.

"Three-year-old body, practically no physical evidence. That's a mess. The theory about the random person, the drifter, that's as good as any."

"But if it's not? If it really was one of the employees at Bubba's?"

"Then you've got yourself a puzzle. And when you've got a puzzle, what do you do? You don't try to solve it all at once. You start on the edges, or wherever's easiest, and you get something to fit. One piece, that's all you need. One piece. And then… one more. You go out there and you find that piece, Hope. Put it in place. The picture will take care of itself. If anyone can do it, Hope, it's you."

~◦ CHAPTER TWENTY-FOUR ◦~

I spent the next two days following Earl's advice. Working the problem. Not trying to solve the whole case at once. Just trying to get one piece of the puzzle to fit.

I chatted with every part-time employee at Bubba's, and found that a lot of them had been there back in Wanda's day. I touched base with all the full-time employees again. I wracked my brain trying to make connections, trying to unearth motives, trying to fit something, anything together.

But come Thursday, I still was no closer to solving my puzzle. Not only had I failed to put any pieces together, I felt like I hadn't even gotten the pieces out of the box.

I needed help.

I needed the whiteboard.

Granny and Bess were arguing about bar peanuts when I dragged the whiteboard down from my apartment and set it up in the middle of the bar.

"Oh, Lordy. Do we have to help you solve another murder?" grumbled Granny.

"You'd rather argue about peanuts?"

"For your information, Bess and I have been arguing about peanuts for thirty years."

Bess confirmed this with a simple nod of the head.

I shrugged. "I know you want me to ask you what the argument's about, but there's nothing I'm less interested in in the entire world."

"I see what you're doing," said Granny. "You're trying to trick us into being interested in *your* thing by showing absolutely no interest in *our* thing."

That was precisely what I was doing. I doubled down. "Honestly, if you paid me to sit around for a week and think of the least interesting topic on earth, I would probably come up with 'Granny and Bess's argument about bar peanuts.'"

"Fine!" said Granny, throwing up her hands. "We'll help you."

The door burst open, and Katie came flying through. "I'll help you too!"

"You look like you're fleeing the authorities."

"Worse. Chris's mother stopped by this morning."

"Then what are you doing here?"

"I told her I had to run an errand."

"You're terrible."

"She's terrible. That woman is blowing up my phone with her texts. Someone should tell her all caps is not a thing anymore."

"Do you really think it's a good idea to make your mother-in-law angry?"

"Are you kidding me? This is the good swift kick in the butt that woman needs to finally become the grandmother I know she can become."

"You mean the kind of grandmother who comes by and watches your children for you?"

"Exactly!" Katie rubbed her hands together. "Okay, let's solve a murder!"

I started by writing Wanda's name in the middle of the whiteboard and then drawing a circle around it.

"For starters," said Granny, "that picture doesn't look anything like Wanda. She wasn't round at all."

Katie agreed. "More like a lumpy rectangle."

"Exactly what I was thinking," Granny said.

I sighed. "I knew it was a mistake to bring the two of you together."

They snickered like they were twelve.

Around the sides of the board, I wrote the names of my suspects, if you could call them that. Kip Granger. Lucinda Meadows. Johnny Driscoll. Mary Riley. Bubba Riley. And then I wrote the word "Other." I drew lines from Wanda to each one of the names. Then I turned around.

"The problem with this murder is simple," I said. "It took place three years ago. We will never know when exactly. We don't know who might or might not have an alibi. And after three years in the pumpkin patch, all that's left of Wanda is a skeleton."

Katie raised her hand. "You think I could get a bumper sticker that says, '*I don't care if your child's an honor student because my kid found some dead lady's arm in a pumpkin patch*'?"

"It's a little wordy," said Granny. "But I like the direction you're going with this."

I ignored them and continued. "The one piece of physical evidence we have is the murder weapon. Wanda was stabbed between the ribs, and the end of the weapon broke off. Unfortunately, not all of it is there, and after this much time, we don't expect there to be fingerprints or DNA evidence."

"What kind of knife was it?" Granny asked.

"That's the interesting part. Initially, Sheriff Kramer told me Wanda was stabbed with a knife. But Dr. Bridges told me that isn't correct. Wanda was stabbed with a flathead screwdriver."

"Then why'd Alex tell you it was a knife?" said Granny.

"Because he doesn't trust me."

"That can't be it," said Katie.

"It is. He knows that's the one detail of the death that only us and the killer know. That secret is leverage against the killer—a way of proving he or she really did do it. Maybe someone slips up and mentions it, and we've got 'em. And Alex thought I'd accidentally leak the information."

"Like you're doing right now," said Granny.

"This is no accident. I'm telling you on purpose."

"Which is totally different," Katie said in her most smart-alecky voice.

I ignored her and pointed at the names on the board. "These names represent our prime suspects—the full-time employees at Bubba's. It could well have been some other person, but Wanda's life was all about the pumpkin patch— that's where she worked, that's where she lived, and she barely came into town. So I've been focusing on the people she knew best: these five people.

"Unfortunately, although I've spoken with them all, and I at least feel like I now know Wanda, I don't feel any closer than when I started to finding the murderer. I don't even have a motive. It's still one big puzzle. And Earl Denton gave me some advice. Don't worry about putting together the whole puzzle, he said. Just start by getting one piece to fit. And that's what I need your help with today."

Katie bounced up and down. "Can we start with the really creepy guy?"

I pointed to the lower right-hand corner of the whiteboard. "Katie's talking about Johnny Driscoll. He's in his late twenties. Has been with Bubba's for seven years. He's some kind of a computer genius. And in addition to helping out with the computer systems at Bubba's, he runs an exhibit called Johnny's Corner. Computerized light shows, robots, that kind of thing."

"And what do you think of him?" Granny asked.

"For about a minute there, in his garage, when I thought his robot might attack me... I thought he might be our guy. He and Wanda had a big rivalry. He thought her old scrap-metal creatures were too old-school. To Johnny Driscoll, they might as well be Muppets. He's into the newest, the sleekest, the high-tech. Wanda didn't share his vision."

"So a good old-fashioned rivalry," said Granny.

"Yep."

"People have killed because of rivalry," Katie added.

"They have."

"But you don't think he did it," said Granny.

205

"No."

Katie frowned. "You haven't ruled him out either."

"No, I haven't."

"How about Lucinda, the donut lady? What's her story?" Granny asked.

"You just said it. Donuts are her story. All it takes is one bite to understand why they won America's Best Donut in 2014. Those apple donuts are incredible. She's also in charge of all the food at Bubba's, and she says she likes to do a little bit of everything around the place. Says it helps understand the best food experience for the visitors.

"Lucinda also gave me the juiciest piece of info so far. Once upon a time, Wanda and Kip Granger were one an item."

"Really?" said Granny.

"She only found out about it after the fact, when Wanda confided in her. All she knows is they dated for a while and Wanda ultimately broke it off."

"And she thinks Kip killed her in some sort of lover's feud?" asked Granny.

"Maybe. Not really. But she also told me that the more she thought about it, Johnny just might be enough of a creep to do it."

"So Lucinda's basically narrowing it down to Johnny or Kip," Katie said.

"Which is exactly what Mary Riley did as well. She thinks that of all the people Wanda argued with, her arguments with Johnny and Kip were the most heated."

"Okay, let's talk about Mary next," said Katie. "What's her story?"

"She's the one who told me all about Bubba's. How they got their start. How they brought Wanda on after that first season. How together, Bubba and Wanda dreamed up a lot of what Bubba's would become. Mary told me it was difficult for many years—that Bubba's dreams were always bigger than their finances. Until, about five years ago… the scales finally tipped. And now, she calls it a miracle."

Granny pointed at the whiteboard. "Mary said Johnny and Kip were the ones who had the most heated arguments with Wanda, but did Mary actually say she thought they may have done it?"

I shook my head. "Nope. Seems like no one honestly suspects anyone. But one thing I found interesting. On that Saturday when the apple of Katie's eye found Wanda's skeleton, Mary and Bubba knew right away it must be Wanda. They said she ran off from time to time. Didn't always see eye to eye with everyone. They figured this time she'd run off for good. Then when the body showed up, they knew it must be her."

"So what?" said Granny.

"There was no hesitation. Bubba and Mary knew right away that it was Wanda."

Granny and Katie exchanged a look.

"There's something else," I said, raising a finger. "I talked to Kip, and he said he remembered Wanda getting into a big argument with Mary right before she went missing, and that it made Wanda really, *really* mad. But then I talked to Bubba, and he said Wanda's fight wasn't with Mary, it was with him."

"And what do you think's going on?" Katie asked.

"My gut feeling? I think someone's lying about that fight. And for whatever reason, I believe Kip. He didn't want to talk initially, but once he did he was open. He admitted to his relationship with Wanda. He obviously didn't trust me, yet he gave me the impression of a man with nothing to hide. Of all the people I spoke to, he's the one I believe the most."

"So you think Bubba is lying," Katie said.

"Yes. I think he was covering for Mary. When I asked him about the fight, he said it was over what the next big exhibit would be. But I'm not buying it. For one thing, Bubba claims that she was mad because he'd firmly decided to build an indoor cafeteria. And I can't help but notice that three years later… Bubba's Pumpkin Patch has no indoor cafeteria."

"Okay, so you think it really was Mary who had the fight with Wanda. Any thoughts as to what the fight was about?" Granny asked.

"I don't have a clue. Maybe that's the first piece of this puzzle that we have to put together."

"I suppose you could just run down to Bubba's and ask him why there's no indoor cafeteria," Granny said.

"And then you can ask Mary what the fight was really about," Katie added.

"I could," I said. "But I'm thinking they're not going to tell me. By now Bubba will have told Mary what he told me. Their story, if it is a story, is established, and they'll both stick to it."

"Then how do we figure it out?" Granny asked.

She and Katie were both silent, which was a minor miracle. Bess was silent because… well, she was Bess. All of us were thinking hard.

Finally, Katie shook her head. "The problem is, we need to know what that argument was about. And the only people who know what it was about are Mary and maybe Bubba. If Wanda had told Lucinda, or Kip, or Johnny, we'd have heard about it. And she wouldn't have told anyone else, because her entire life was at that pumpkin patch. It's too bad she didn't have a sister, or somebody she confided in."

As Katie spoke, Granny's face changed. Like she remembered something. She turned to Bess, and the two of them exchanged a look. I'd seen that look a thousand times in my life. They'd exchanged information.

Granny turned back to me and let out an uncomfortable breath. "It's possible that there were some people outside of Bubba's who at one point were pretty close with Wanda."

"Who?"

"The people who attended our monthly poker game."

"Monthly poker game? Why do I not know about a monthly poker game?"

"Because I never told you about it before."

"Why? It's just poker."

"Well, it is and it isn't. I didn't want to have to tell you just how much money I was gambling. You see, the poker game I'm talking about… it was high stakes. And Wanda was a regular."

⌒ CHAPTER TWENTY-FIVE ⌒

I pointed my finger at Granny. "You!" Then I swung it at Bess. "And you!"

Both of them looked down at the floor.

"I can't *believe* this!" I shouted. "You knew Wanda! She was in your regular poker game! And you didn't think of telling me this on Sunday when we talked about the case at Buck's?"

Granny raised her hands. "No, I *did* think about it. I just didn't *do* it. And there's a reason for that."

"This better be good."

"Trust me, it is. Remember that fighting movie with Brad Pitt?"

"What?"

"You know, Brad Pitt, that sexy guy who was married to the skinny chick with the big lips."

"I know who Brad Pitt is, Granny."

"He's got that movie about men beating the crap out of each other."

"*Fight Club*?"

"That's the one. Well, we don't know how they did it, but we're pretty sure *Fight Club* did some serious copyright infringement when they made that movie."

"I am so confused."

"Do you know what the first rule of Poker Night is? You guessed it. The first rule of Poker Night is that you *do not talk about Poker Night*. It's one of those ironclad kind of rules. Listen, Hope, if this were some chump-change poker game, I would have told you a long time ago. But I'm not talking about chump change. People can win a lot of money at our games…" She made a face. "And they can lose a lot of money."

"Define a lot. Fifty bucks?"

Granny shook her head.

"A hundred?"

Now Granny just looked uncomfortable.

"A *thousand*?"

She shrugged. So did Bess.

"*More* than a thousand dollars?"

Granny waved her hands back and forth. "But never more than ten."

"*TEN THOUSAND DOLLARS?* Are you *insane*?"

"In our defense, the reaction you're having is the whole reason we don't talk about the game in the first place. Also, I'm pretty sure it's illegal. And to be honest, when we first heard about Wanda, Bess and I assumed the poker game didn't have anything to do with her murder."

"And now?" I asked.

Granny let out a big sigh. "Now I'm not so sure."

The thought of Granny sitting around, smoking cigars, and playing poker with other old ladies was not at all odd. In fact, it suited her. But the thought of her playing poker for *thousands of dollars…* that blew my mind.

"Why do you play for so much money?" Katie asked.

"It didn't start out that way. But over time, the stakes just grew. I don't know… when you're old and your joints don't work, there's only so much you can do to feel alive and… on the edge." She shrugged. "This is one way to live on the edge."

"But what if you lose big?" I asked. "Couldn't you go broke?"

"It doesn't happen. We're all fairly even players, so over time, the winning and losing balances out."

"But it *could* happen," said Katie.

"Sure, but we're big girls. We know what we're getting into."

I couldn't believe this. My own grandmother was a regular participant in a crazy high-stakes poker game. Not to mention Bess. But I couldn't think about this right now. I had to focus on the murder investigation.

And on the witness who had been withholding evidence.

"Okay, Granny, your secret's out now, so spill. Obviously you think this poker game might have something to do with Wanda's death. Tell me how."

"I'm not saying that! But I'll tell you what I know. About three years ago, Wanda stopped playing in our monthly game."

"I imagine it's difficult to play poker when you're dead," Katie said.

"No, smart aleck, before that. She didn't come to our poker night one night, even though I had seen her driving through town earlier that day. I asked Flo why Wanda wasn't playing, and she said Wanda wouldn't be back. When we asked why, Flo said she didn't want to talk about it."

Flo was in on this too? So many questions. But I stuck to the case.

"And you just left it at that?" I asked.

"Well, I was working on a straight flush for a five-hundred-dollar pot at the time, so I was a little distracted."

"And that was it? Your poker buddy Wanda was gone forever, and you never followed up with Flo about it."

"Well, 'buddy' is a strong word. Wanda was a regular. That's about it. And then she wasn't. For a bunch of old ladies who've experienced our fair share of loss, a missing Wanda really wasn't that big of a deal."

"But now you think she was murdered because of your secret, irresponsible poker game."

"Stop putting words in my mouth! I said nothing of the sort. *You* said we need to start by putting in one piece of the puzzle. And this is a piece, isn't it? I never did find out from Flo why Wanda didn't come to our game that night."

"And now?"

"I think it's time we find out."

Granny, Bess, Katie, and I all took seats inside Flo's Beauty Parlor while Flo locked the door, put the closed sign in the window, and lowered the shades. Flo then turned to Granny and Bess and shook her head in disappointment.

"I didn't have a choice!" said Granny. "It's a murder investigation."

"Well, the deed is done," said Flo. "Do we have them take the blood oath?"

"What's the blood oath?" Katie asked.

Flo leaned forward. "It's where you take a knife, slice your palm, and let the blood drip into a little dish while you promise to never, ever talk about Poker Night. And for the record, the blood oath used to mean something around here." She shot Granny a look.

"It's a *murder investigation*!" Granny yelled. "And we haven't made anyone take the blood oath in years. I say you make them drink the hooch."

Katie and I exchanged a look, then in unison we said, "The hooch?"

Flo pulled out her keys and unlocked a wooden cabinet in the corner of her shop. She pulled out what looked like a moonshine jug from a comic strip, along with two glasses. She filled the glasses and brought them over to me and Katie.

"Do you promise to never, ever talk about Poker Night?" she said. She spoke in a tone I had never, ever heard from Flo before.

"Do we really have to promise?" Katie asked.

"You either make the promise, or I'm not giving you any information."

Katie and I grabbed the little shot glasses. "I promise to never ever talk about Poker Night," I said.

Katie nodded. "Ditto."

Then we threw back our hooch.

For the first half second, I thought I was going to be okay. Then the real power of the hooch kicked in. I was on the floor, on my hands and knees, coughing like my throat had just been attacked by an army of demons.

Katie was right there with me, her eyes watering. "Is this what death feels like, Hope?"

I didn't want to use what little energy I had to open my mouth. But Katie had it right. I was pretty sure this was what death felt like.

I stumbled to my feet, went over to one of Flo's sinks, and splashed water on my face. Then I stuck the little hair-washing wand in my mouth and sprayed. That felt better.

It took us a few minutes to regain full control of our faculties. And I promised myself, if I were ever again given the choice between slicing my hand with a knife or taking the hooch... I would bleed like a stuck pig.

"You two done rolling around like a couple of sissies?" Granny said.

"What in holy hell is in that stuff?" asked Katie, massaging her throat with both hands.

"By the taste of it, you'd think it was a combination of gasoline and Tabasco sauce, wouldn't you?" said Flo.

"Please tell me it's not *actually* a combination of gasoline and Tabasco sauce," I said.

Flo winked. "Okay, it's not actually a combination of gasoline and Tabasco sauce."

Katie dug her fingernails into my forearm. "Oh dear God, we're going to die."

Flo sat down in her beauty chair and folded her hands in her lap, the tips of her fingers tapping against each other. Somehow sweet Flo the hairdresser had been transformed into a hard-edged Mafia don.

"So what do you want to know about Poker Night?" she said.

"We understand Wanda Wegman was a part of Poker Night," I said.

"She was."

"And that around three years ago, shortly before we think she was murdered… she stopped coming to Poker Night."

"That's right."

Granny leaned forward. "Flo, what we want to know is, why did Wanda stop coming? I never asked you at the time, but I'm asking you now."

Flo's eyes widened. "I didn't murder her. Are you saying I murdered her?"

"No, no," I said. "It never crossed my mind. We're just trying to better understand what Wanda was up to right around the time of her murder. Hopefully, it can give us a lead."

Flo looked uncertain.

"So why did Wanda stop coming?" Granny asked again.

"Because… I told her not to come back."

"What? Why?" I said.

Flo hesitated, then she climbed off of her chair and walked back to that cabinet in the corner. She pulled out a metal box, rifled through it, and took out an envelope. She handed that envelope to me.

"Because of this," she said.

I opened the envelope and pulled out a twenty-dollar bill inside a clear plastic sleeve. I held it up so Granny, Bess, and Katie could all see it.

"You asked her not to come back because of a twenty-dollar bill?"

Flo sat back down on her chair. "I've been running a small business since forever, and every once in a while, I'll take a class or go to a conference to learn what I can. Several years ago, I took a one-day class in Boise on fraud. It covered things like bad checks, credit card swipers, and counterfeit money. I found the whole thing fascinating—especially the business about counterfeit money—and by the end of the day, I got pretty good at spotting fakes. So after that, I routinely inspected the bills that came through my shop to see if they were legit."

"And were they?" Katie asked.

"Almost always, yes. But every once in a while, a counterfeit bill shows up. Not from a counterfeiter, mind you. I've done a little extra research on the subject, and it's amazing how much counterfeit money is floating around our country."

"And this particular twenty is a counterfeit?" I asked.

"It is," Flo said, "and it came from Wanda. I'm not sure what Granny has already told you about our game."

"Just that it's monthly and it's pretty high-stakes," I said.

"And the stakes are high enough that we have a gentlewoman's agreement: a player has until the following month to pay off her debt. That gives people a chance to get a paycheck or Social Security benefits…"

"Or sell an organ," said Katie.

"Precisely," said Flo without even flinching. "Anyway it just so happens that three years ago and some change, I won a significant amount of money from Wanda."

"How significant?" I asked.

"In the neighborhood of two grand. A little under a month later, Wanda gave me the money in cash. And, as had become my custom, I started examining the money right there."

"And you found this fake twenty-dollar bill," I said.

Flo shook her head. "No. I found *many* fake twenty-dollar bills."

"How many?"

"*All* of them. The entire two thousand dollars was counterfeit."

Katie gasped. "What did you do?"

"I got angry. I gave her one week to give me real money, and I told her never to come back to our poker game. It seems our Wanda was more than a pumpkin patch worker who was hard to get along with." Flo folded her arms. "Wanda Wegman was a counterfeiter."

～CHAPTER TWENTY-SIX ～

Thirty minutes later, Mary Riley unlocked the door to Wanda Wegman's cottage so I could have another look around.

"Anything in particular you're looking for this time?" Mary asked.

"No, nothing in particular. Just hoping to get lucky."

"Well, I've got to get back to work, so I'll leave you to it. Please let me know if there's anything more Bubba and I can do. We all want to find whoever did this to poor Wanda."

Of course, *nothing in particular* wasn't the truth. If Wanda Wegman was a counterfeiter, I was hoping to find something that would prove it.

I searched the cottage once again—but far more thoroughly this time. I looked under beds, inside dresser drawers, and inside every cabinet I could find. I even poked my head up into the attic, using my phone as a flashlight. There was nothing out of the ordinary. Nothing to suggest that Wanda Wegman was printing fake money.

Then I stopped and looked at the computer on her desk

in her room, and I wondered. How exactly does one learn how to make counterfeit money?

How does one learn to do anything these days?

The internet.

I made sure the cord was plugged in, then turned on the computer. As it started going through its bootup procedure, I decided this would be easier with a little help.

I placed a call.

"Hey, big sexy!" I said with as much enthusiasm as I could muster.

"Big sexy?" said Darwin in his usual boring drawl.

"Would you prefer 'little sexy'?"

"What do you want, Hope?"

"I take it you don't have any results for me on the package I sent you?"

"I told you I'd never done that before."

"Which is not the same as you not being able to do it. So—were you able to do it?"

"Well, yes. But that's not the point."

"What is the point, darling?"

"That you just expect me to move heaven and earth for you at the drop of a hat. I feel underappreciated."

"I called you big sexy and darling, and you feel underappreciated?"

"I feel like you're teasing me."

"Darwin, I'm going to make you a deal. You drive to Hopeless, Idaho, and I will take you out to dinner at this great place I know that serves free peanuts. And if you play your cards right, at the end of our date, I'll even kiss you goodnight."

There was silence on the other end of the line. A long, uncomfortable silence.

"Darwin, are you okay?"

"You're not still teasing, are you?"

"Nope. You show up in Hopeless, and it's a date. I'll wear clean underwear, put on deodorant, the works."

"Okay," he finally said. "It's a date."

"Great. Now, what exactly is your update on the package?"

"Well, I was actually going to call you later with my update. I wanted to check my results again."

"You never struck me as a check-your-results kind of guy."

"I'm not, usually… but this time I feel like something must be wrong."

"Why?"

"The fingerprints you found have no match… but the DNA does. The DNA belongs to a woman named Samantha Jones."

"So Ms. Jones really *was* her real name."

"Well, just wait. The only thing I could find about Samantha Jones was she's the owner of an independent real estate consultant business called Happy Farms Real Estate. It's owned by another business, an LLC called Portland Sunrise, LLC. And Hope, I don't think these are real companies. They're clearly shells."

"And what's behind these shells?"

"This is the part you're not going to believe."

"Try me."

"According to the records I found, these companies are owned entirely by another company. And its name is... Hope Walker Enterprises."

My jaw dropped. "Is this some kind of a joke?"

"Not by me. But Hope, somebody went to a lot of trouble to do this."

"Which means?"

"Someone is messing with you."

That much was clear. Somebody *knew* I would look into Ms. Jones... and this was their message. A message meant for me. The message was simple.

I'm smarter than you.

And at least for the moment, they were right.

Wanda's computer brought up the desktop, and I was reminded why I called Darwin in the first place.

"Okay, Darwin, I have another request for you. A much easier one. I need help accessing some information on a computer."

"That seems like the kind of thing you could handle yourself, Hope."

"But you can handle it so much better. I just turned this computer on for the first time in three years. It belonged to a woman named Wanda Wegman, and I'm investigating her death. I want her search histories, especially the last couple months of her life. I want access to her emails. Anything."

"You have access to the computer?"

"It's right in front of me."

"Can you get on the internet?"

"Let me see." I searched for Wi-Fi networks, found one

called Bubba's Patch Public, and logged on. "Okay, I'm on."

"I need you to type 'remotedarwin.com' into the search bar."

"Give me a second." I opened up Chrome, typed in the domain name, and clicked. A site popped up with a square in the middle.

"Now type the following password into the box." Darwin gave me a series of nine letters and numbers, which I dutifully entered.

"Okay," Darwin said, "I'm in."

"You mean you're in this computer?"

"Yep, I've got total control."

"Sweet. How long will it take you to get what I need?"

"I already have it. You should see an archived history of her internet search on your screen. Told you you could do this, Hope. There's nothing tricky about pulling up a search history."

"Yes, but I like it better when you do it."

Darwin sighed. "Do you need anything else?"

"I might… but this is good for now. Thanks, Darwin."

I got off the phone and checked Wanda's history. Her last search was just over three years ago, once again confirming the time of her disappearance. I wrote down the date on a pad of paper, then I started perusing the types of things Wanda had been looking at.

Most of it was ordinary stuff. Or at least, ordinary stuff for someone like Wanda. Baking websites. Recipes. Mechanical sites. Something about welding. Websites for a couple of other pumpkin patches. *But*—sprinkled throughout all of this was something else.

Searches about counterfeiting.

Bingo.

I opened all of the searches into different tabs and started skimming to find out what Wanda was learning about. Taken together, the dozen or so pages I read through were like a crash course on how to make fake money. The type of paper to use. The type of ink and where to get it. The types of color laser printers that worked best. And on and on and on. After reading all of it, I was actually thinking about counterfeiting money myself. It truly was extraordinary what you could learn on the internet.

But though the knowledge-gathering was easy, the actual doing of it did not seem easy at all. You had to find and buy just the right paper, the right ink, the right machines, and you had to develop the artistry to actually do it. Learnable, yes. Easy? Not a chance.

And that's when something struck me. The searches about counterfeiting were all in the last two weeks of her search history. I double-checked—went back further in time and worked my back up to her most recent internet usage. There was no doubt about it: there was not a single search on any counterfeiting topics until the final two weeks of her search history. Presumably the last two weeks of her life.

Hard to believe that Wanda learned how to print fake money, and then successfully printed a huge batch of it, all in the course of two weeks.

Which meant…

Flo was wrong. Wanda wasn't a counterfeiter.

But somebody else was.

And Wanda had been trying to figure it out.

～～ CHAPTER TWENTY-SEVEN ～～

One of the searches in Wanda's history was for the Secret Service. I always thought of the Secret Service as being the people who protect the president and other dignitaries, but it turns out they also have a huge role in combating fraud—including the counterfeiting of money.

So I found the contact info for the Boise branch of the Secret Service and called it. I thought they might be able to help me figure out who was behind the fake money. The secretary forwarded me on to one of the agents in charge.

"Special Agent Rebecca Vargas. How can I help you?"

I told Special Agent Vargas that I was an investigative reporter with confidential sources who was working on a story about counterfeiting.

"Right there in Hopeless?" she said.

"You know Hopeless?"

"I'm familiar with it. So—exactly how can I help you with your story?"

"Well, basically, I was handed a twenty-dollar bill that I'm told is a counterfeit. My source said this particular twenty was part of two thousand dollars in counterfeit bills that was handed to her a few years back as payment for a debt."

"And I suppose you're not going to tell me where it came from."

"No, I'm not going to tell you my source. But if I can figure out where the counterfeit bills came from, I *will* tell you that."

She paused, then finally let out a breath. "Okay, I'm intrigued. What more can you share?"

I started at the beginning. From finding Wanda's body to looking at Wanda's search history, I told Agent Vargas everything I could... except for the part about the illegal high-stakes poker game and a certain hairdresser and bar owner who played in it. When I was done, I asked for her opinion.

"First, I think you're right about Wanda. She's not your girl. The internet can teach you about counterfeiting, but doing it is a whole 'nother thing. Sounds to me like she discovered some counterfeit money and decided to investigate it herself."

"Okay, then help me out. She comes into two thousand dollars that she uses to pay off a debt—and then she's surprised to learn that the money is fake. My question is, where would two thousand dollars in cash come from? Could it be from a bank withdrawal?"

"Doubtful. Most banks, even small-town banks, have electronic cash counters for bigger stacks of money. These counters also have scanners that scan for bad bills.

Counterfeit money rarely shows up in banks because they catch it on either the deposit or the withdrawal."

"What are the other options?" I asked.

"She could have been given a gift. Or… there's one other possibility that comes to mind. I don't see it that often, but it would explain the large amount of money." Special Agent Vargas explained to me what she was thinking.

"Any thoughts on how I might confirm that?" I asked.

"I think you need to ask those employees one more question."

Then, to my surprise, Special Agent Vargas offered to come to Hopeless and take a look into this if I wanted. "Murder, counterfeit money, an old lady, and a crazy pumpkin patch? Ms. Walker, this sounds way more interesting than most of the things I usually get to deal with. So if you need me, just call. I can be there within the hour."

"Thank you, Agent Vargas. I will definitely keep that offer in mind."

I visited Johnny's Corner first. Johnny was just finishing up a dazzling display with his robot, and it was clear that the kids absolutely loved it. Even I had to admit that, though there were no flying chunks of pumpkin to avoid, it was still extremely cool.

Next I talked to Kip Granger down at the corn maze. He had just finished sending a group of kids screaming into the maze—better them than me—and was happy to give me a moment of his time.

I found Lucinda Meadows working the counter at Lucinda's Famous Apple Donuts. I bought three more warm donuts while I was there.

And at each stop, I asked the same two questions.

Do you think Wanda might be printing fake money?

And…

Did Bubba's ever pay you in cash?

For the first question, they all had the same answer: *No way.* When it came to Wanda Wegman, the one thing everyone agreed on—besides that she was difficult—was that she was honest. In fact, those two personality traits were closely intertwined. Wanda was no cheat. She was not our counterfeiter.

The second question caught them off guard, but again, their answers were largely the same: *Yes.* Johnny said he'd been paid in cash several times, but not for a while. Kip agreed. Said it had been maybe three years.

Lucinda didn't need to guess when it happened last. She said she'd look at her records.

"You kept records of how you were paid?"

She sat down at her computer in a cramped office at the back of her kitchen. "Not as such, but I have a record of all my bank deposits. And… any time I was paid cash… I didn't deposit it."

"Why not?"

"Isn't it obvious? If I don't deposit it, I don't have to claim it as income, and I don't have to pay taxes on it. I hate taxes."

She looked through her records. "Okay, looks like the

last time we were paid cash was a little over…"

"Three years ago?" I said.

She smiled. "Yeah. How did you know?"

On my way out, I grabbed another warm apple donut. I took a big bite as I called Special Agent Vargas.

"You were right," I said.

"Then Bubba's Pumpkin Patch, here I come. I'll be there as soon as I can."

There was one more call I needed to make. A call I'd been avoiding since Monday. But he was the sheriff, and I couldn't do what I was about to do without him.

He answered after the first ring.

"Hello, Hope."

"Hi, Alex."

"I'm really sorry," he said.

"I got angry."

"I know. And I understand why."

"Do you?"

"I think I do."

"Were we having dinner that night just so we could compare notes on the case?"

"I hope not," he said.

"What do you mean?"

"I mean… I was hoping it was more than that."

My heart fluttered. But I also got angry. Again.

"Then why did you kiss her?"

"I didn't kiss her, Hope. She kissed me."

"Then why did you *let* her kiss you? She's Gemima Clark. She's a walking cliché of a homewrecker. She has spent my entire life trying to make my life miserable. Why did you have to let her kiss you?"

He said nothing.

"And Alex, when you arrested me... you embarrassed me... in front of everyone."

"But you punched her."

"And she kissed you without you ever asking for it. You could have told her that, in front of everyone. You could have refused to arrest me like I was some common criminal. So why did you?"

"I... I don't know, Hope. I was embarrassed. I didn't know what to do. All I can say is... I'm sorry."

"Thank you," I said. "Think we can we start over?"

"You want to go out to dinner and compare notes on our investigation again?"

"Something like that. But the comparing of notes is going to have to wait. That's why I was calling you. I need you to come out to Bubba's. I just solved the case and I need you to make the arrest."

"You what? What are you talking about?"

"I'm talking about the killer, Alex. I know who killed Wanda Wegman."

↷ CHAPTER TWENTY-EIGHT ↶

As I waited for the cavalry outside the big barn at the front entrance to Bubba's, I made a late-afternoon call to Stephen Dinsdale at the Hopeless Bank and Trust. In high school, everyone called him "Booger"; the main thing I remembered about him was that he always had the hots for Katie. Nowadays, everybody called him "Mr. Vice President," and he had a brand-new house outside of town. Thankfully, he was happy to answer a few of my questions. They only confirmed my conclusion.

When Sheriff Kramer arrived, he looked uneasy. "Is this going to be another example of you throwing around crazy murder allegations with absolutely no proof?"

"Why of course. I do have a reputation to uphold, Sheriff. But there will be one distinct difference this time."

"What's that?"

"I'm going to have leverage."

"How so?"

I nodded to a woman who was just walking toward us. She wore a light-gray suit jacket and pants over a black blouse. She had long black hair, olive skin, and dark but beautiful eyes. A badge was attached to her waist.

"That's my leverage," I said.

Alex turned to look at her—and as soon as he did, his body language instantly changed. So did the special agent's. She stopped suddenly and her eyes widened.

"Rebecca?" said Sheriff Kramer. "What are you doing here?"

Agent Vargas smiled. "I wondered if you'd be here."

"The two of you know each other?" I said.

Agent Vargas gave Alex a funny look, then smiled. "We used to work together at the state police."

Alex's eyes darted between Rebecca and me. "Wait, *you* called Rebecca?"

"I called the Secret Service."

Vargas raised her hand. "And I answered."

Alex was clearly confused. "And now you're here... to...?"

"Hopefully arrest someone for counterfeiting," said Agent Vargas. "And who knows, maybe you can catch a murderer at the same time."

Watching the two of them, I felt suddenly uneasy. There was something about the way they reacted to each other. And especially, about the way Alex reacted to her. She was beautiful... and he was nervous. Maybe Alex Kramer and Rebecca Vargas had been *more* than just work colleagues.

Alex's snapping fingers brought me back to life. "Hope, do you have an actual plan?"

"Um, me, plan."

"Yes," said Alex. "A plan."

"Do either of you happen to have a polygraph machine with you?" I asked.

They both shook their heads. "No."

"Then I don't have a plan. But don't worry. I'm pretty good at winging it."

"Do either of us have a role in this plan of yours?" Alex asked.

"Just look mean. And if you're carrying a gun… make sure they see it."

When I'd chatted with the employees this week, one of the things I'd learned was that all the full-time employees, along with the most important of the part-time and seasonal workers, had an "All-Patch Meeting" with Bubba and Mary every Friday afternoon. And sure enough, I found them all gathered in the large office space beside the main entrance.

As I walked in, Bubba was slapping his hands together. "Remember, starting tonight things go into overdrive. More cars. More people. More everything. Keep your cool, and no matter what, smile. These people spend a lot of good hard-earned money to come out to the pumpkin patch, and they deserve our best."

Then Bubba looked up and saw me—along with Sheriff Kramer and Special Agent Vargas. His eyes flickered with confusion. "Hope? Sheriff? Um, is there something we can do for you?"

I smiled. "I apologize, Bubba. Mary. We just wanted to give you an update on the case."

"Oh, that's great. But, um, we're in the middle of a staff meeting," Bubba said.

"And that will have to wait," said Sheriff Kramer. "We have important news."

Kip stood. "Did you find out who killed her?"

Johnny gave Agent Vargas a rather obvious once-over. "More importantly, who's she?"

Super creepy.

"Her name is Rebecca Vargas," I said, "and I'll come back to her in a bit."

I walked into the center of the room. I felt like a lawyer at the end of a big case. I just hoped I could deliver.

"I've talked with all of you in this room. Some multiple times. And most of you told me that you just can't imagine anyone killing Wanda. I believe you. It is hard to imagine. Unless you understand the reason."

"The motive," said Bubba.

I pointed to him. "Exactly. That's what I focused on this week. Who had the best reason, the strongest motive to kill Wanda?"

"And what did you find out?" Mary asked.

"Well, one thing I heard over and over again was that Wanda could be difficult."

The crowd murmured in agreement.

"She was smart, and she liked to let you know she was smart. She had strong ideas about how things should be done around here, and she didn't back down. She argued with Bubba… a lot. She argued with Mary. And with Lucinda. But arguing… being difficult … is not a very strong reason for murder.

"She also had a rival. Johnny. Someone who, like Wanda, is very smart."

"A genius, really," he said from the crowd.

"I stand corrected. Johnny is a genius. Two geniuses with competing visions. Rivals. Is that a reason for murder? Maybe."

"What do you mean maybe?" Johnny objected.

"How about 'definite maybe'?"

Johnny nodded as if this was more acceptable.

"What other motives are there for murder? How about… a broken heart?" I turned to Kip Granger. "Kip had no particular grievance with Wanda… in fact, at one time Kip and Wanda were an item. Until Wanda dumped him. Did a lover's quarrel develop into a violent, jealous rage? It's been known to happen."

Kip grunted. "Didn't though."

"Or… was there no motive at all, other than the joy of killing? Is it possible that the murderer was some random drifter off the street who didn't even know Wanda—but just felt like killing? Maybe Wanda was simply in the wrong place at the wrong time. I know lots of people here think that's what really happened. And I know for certain that the real killer is *hoping* that's what we'll believe."

I turned in place, gradually surveying everyone in the room.

"Ladies and gentlemen, the truth is… Wanda's killer *did* have a motive to kill her. A very, very *strong* motive."

I gestured toward Special Agent Vargas. "I think now a good time to tell you a little bit more about this woman with the badge and the gun. I told you her name is Rebecca Vargas, and that's true. What I didn't tell you is she normally goes by 'Special Agent Vargas,' and she works for the Secret Service."

A murmur went through the room.

"Yes, *that* Secret Service. The one that's in charge of protecting the President of the United States—and also in charge of protecting our nation's money supply."

The noose was tightening. By now the killer knew where I was going with this. I was glad Alex was here to back me up.

"Wanda Wegman died because she discovered something. She discovered that someone here at Bubba's was printing counterfeit money. About three years ago—and about two weeks before her death, Bubba's Pumpkin Patch paid her in cash. She used that cash to pay off a debt to a friend. And when she did, the friend discovered the money was fake."

"What?" came a chorus of voices from the crowd.

"Not just some of it. Not a stray bill here and there. *All* of it was fake," I said. "The friend thought Wanda was a fraud. Wanda, as you can well believe, was mortified at being called dishonest. You all knew this about Wanda. She wouldn't let you cheat at cards. She wouldn't let you cheat at anything. And the idea that somebody thought she was a fraud? That somebody thought she was a cheat? Well, that made her furious.

"So she spent the next couple of weeks—the last two weeks of her life, in fact—learning everything she could about counterfeiting. And then Wanda—honest, difficult Wanda—went to *confront* the person who gave her the counterfeit money in the first place. Or more specifically, the person who *paid* her the counterfeit money. As part of her paycheck.

"You see, a few years ago, Bubba's Pumpkin Patch would occasionally pay its employees in cash. The explanation was always that Bubba's was a cash business, and besides, no one objected—you don't have to claim it for taxes, right? But the real reason was quite different.

"Bubba Riley always wanted Bubba's to be more than it was… and much more than it could afford to be. He never did understand the finances or how they worked; his wife did all that. It was Mary who was always working hard to keep them, and this place, and all of you, above water. But no matter how tight the money was, all Bubba wanted to do was grow. Be bigger. Be better. And then one day, maybe four or five years ago… Mary came upon a solution: counterfeit money."

I turned to Mary. "I'm guessing you realized that a place like Bubba's was the perfect spot to use counterfeit money. You deal with enormous amounts of cash, and it's disbursed broadly among many thousands of people. You probably realized that large amounts of fake money are relatively easy to spot, but an extra twenty here or there? Not so much. And maybe it never would have been spotted—if you hadn't, occasionally, used it to pay your employees. My guess is you didn't want to do that. My guess is you did that only when times were especially tight. But it cost you. Because one day, one of those employees discovered the truth."

"What are you saying?" said Bubba.

"I'm saying that Wanda Wegman confronted your wife,

Bubba. Wanda had discovered that Mary was a counterfeiter, and Wanda was going to turn her in. Mary was going to go to jail. *Unless…* unless she could stop Wanda. Somehow.

"And that brings us to our final motive: *avoiding prison.* I'd say that's about as strong a motive as you'll ever find. And that's exactly why Mary Riley killed Wanda."

"That's insane!" said Bubba.

But Mary's face, a twisted wreck of a face, said something different. "You've got no proof," she said.

"That's where Special Agent Vargas comes in."

Vargas stepped into the middle of the room. She looked mean. She made sure people saw her gun. She focused her eyes on Mary.

"Ma'am, I've already examined the twenty-dollar bill that came from you. It's a fake, and a pretty good one at that. Based on that and the story I've heard, I have the authority to shut Bubba's down immediately, pending an investigation of the cash currency on hand. Right now. Mary and Bubba Riley, I'm going to go through every inch of your life, and I promise you, I will find out every single bit there is to this story. And the more I find, the longer your prison sentence will be." She paused. "Or…"

"Or?" said Mary.

"Or… you cooperate. You may have funneled a lot of counterfeit currency through this place, but I'm guessing you didn't print it yourself. I think there's a bigger fish out there… and if you lead me to them, then maybe I can make a deal."

"You'd make a deal for murder?" Kip said.

"I'm just interested in the counterfeiting. You'll have to talk to the sheriff about the murder."

Bubba's eyes shifted to Sheriff Kramer.

"I can't make deals on murder," said the sheriff. "But if Mary cooperates… if she admits what she did, and if the judge is convinced it was a tragic mistake and not premeditated… that will likely be reflected in a reduced sentence. And maybe one day, in fifteen or twenty years, Mary can get a second chance."

Bubba looked at his wife. "What do you think, Mary?"

"What do I think? What do I *think*? Bubba, I made some mistakes—I admit that. But I did *not* kill Wanda Wegman!"

Alex looked at me and shook his head. "Why is it they rarely come quietly?"

Special Agent Vargas walked up to Mary and pulled out her handcuffs. "Mary Riley, you're under arrest."

And all five foot two inches of Mary Riley screamed.

～CHAPTER TWENTY-NINE ～

Mary and Bubba Riley were escorted to the Hopeless jail by Sheriff Alex Kramer and Special Agent Rebecca Vargas. Bubba was put into a quiet room in the back while the sheriff and the special agent led the interrogation of the prime suspect. I was lucky enough to be an interested bystander.

Now that she was off of her home turf, Mary completely broke down. She confessed to the charge of counterfeiting. She explained that five years ago, things were bad at Bubba's. Really bad. Business had picked up, but Bubba's dreams were expensive. They were always eating away their profits—and more. A part-time worker named Alice was helping Mary in the office that season, and Alice mentioned she might know someone who could help out. That led to a contact with a man named Derby Sledge. Mary would contact Derby through a simple text message. Derby would meet her, sell her a bag of counterfeit money for ten cents on the dollar, and Mary would take it back to Bubba's. She started off by adding it to the money supply at Bubba's gradually, so as not to cause suspicion. But there were times, when things were particularly bad, when she would use the cash to meet payroll.

In the end, Mary shared every detail of the operation. And she promised to help them nail Derby to the wall.

And finally, that brought them to the untimely death of Wanda Wegman.

"Did Wanda confront you?" the sheriff asked.

"Yes."

"Was she angry?"

"Of course."

"Did she threaten to turn you in?"

"Absolutely."

"And that's when you killed her?"

"No." Mary was defiant. "I didn't kill her."

"Then what happened?"

"She demanded that I pay her with genuine cash immediately, and she made me promise to never every use counterfeit money ever again."

"Or else…?"

"Or else she would turn me in to the sheriff."

"And that's when you killed her?" Alex asked again.

"I told you: I didn't kill her."

"So who *did* kill her?"

"I have no idea!" Mary exclaimed.

And on it went like this for the next hour. Finally, Alex and Rebecca came out and met me.

"She's lying, right?"

"Probably," said Alex. "Doing time for counterfeiting is much better than doing time for murder."

"And she's got no incentive to tell us the truth," Rebecca added.

"What are you getting at?"

"Maybe we should give her one."

The three of us joined Bubba in an interview room. I stood against the wall, while the sheriff and the special agent sat at a wooden table with Bubba. They calmly but firmly laid out the entire case against Mary, and they told him what she had admitted to. He was absolutely heartbroken.

"But," said Alex, "she's denying having anything to do with the murder of Wanda."

"Of course she is. Mary could never murder anyone."

Agent Vargas raised an eyebrow. "And earlier today, you probably didn't think your wife could deal in counterfeit money. People can surprise you."

"Mary could never hurt anyone!"

"I don't think a jury is going to see it that way," Alex said. "The jury will learn that Mary was involved in a crooked counterfeiting operation. The jury will learn that Wanda discovered Mary's secret. We don't have to prove any of that, Mr. Riley—Mary has already confessed to all of it. And everyone who knew Wanda will testify, with certainty, that Wanda would have exposed Mary. Would have sent her to jail for a very long time. And coincidentally, right after that confrontation, Wanda ended up dead. See, Mr. Riley, we don't have to have proof of murder. We just have to tell the jury a story. And that… is a pretty compelling story."

"Y-you can't do this," Bubba spluttered.

"We can, and we will," said Alex. "Unless… there's any chance that someone else killed Wanda Wegman?"

Bubba's eyes widened.

"Think about it, Mr. Riley," said Agent Vargas. "A woman as small as Mary? A woman with Mary's temperament? How do you think she's going to fare in a supermax prison?"

Bubba buried his face in his hands. "Not very well."

"So, that brings us to one important question," Alex said. "Are you really going to let your wife take the blame for something *you* did?"

Bubba's head snapped up. "What?"

"You already protected your wife from going to prison once, Bubba. When Wanda threated to expose her, you just couldn't let that happen to your Mary. So you protected her the only way you could. And now you can protect her again, by telling us the truth. It was you who killed Wanda Wegman, wasn't it?"

Bubba put his chin to his chest and sobbed. Great, heaving sobs. Finally he sniffled and looked up at Alex. "Yes, it was me."

As Alex took Bubba into custody, I leaned in toward Rebecca. "Okay, I understood the plan, but now I'm unsure. Bubba didn't *really* do it, did he?"

Rebecca shook her head. "Nah, he's just covering for his wife, like we thought he would."

"It felt kind of mean," I said.

She winked. "Yep. But now we have a powerful incentive for his wife to confess the truth."

Minutes later, Alex, Rebecca, and I had rejoined Mary, and Rebecca explained to Mary what had just happened.

Mary howled. "No!" she screamed. "Bubba didn't do it! He couldn't have!"

"And how could you know that?" the special agent asked.

"Because..." She took a deep breath, and her expression changed to one of desperate determination. "Because *I* did it. I killed Wanda Wegman. You're right about everything. She confronted me. She made me promise not to use counterfeit money anymore, and I did. But she was going to turn me in anyway. And then I... and then I just lost my mind. I grabbed that knife and I stabbed her. I did it. Bubba had nothing to do with it."

Special Agent Vargas smiled, first at Alex and then at me. "Looks like you just solved your murder case."

But I wasn't so sure.

I stepped forward. "Tell me again, Mary, what you did. How exactly did you kill Wanda? I know this is hard, but we need details."

"Well... I was mad. So mad. And scared. And the knife was there, and I grabbed it and I stabbed her with it. And then I buried her in the pumpkin patch."

"Just like that?" Alex said.

She nodded. "Just like that."

Special Agent Vargas smiled at us again. "Seems pretty clear cut to me."

Alex shook his head, then he motioned for Agent Vargas and me to follow him out of the room and down the hall. Then he turned to us both and said, "We have a problem."

"I picked up on that," said Rebecca. "What's the problem?"

"Wanda Wegman was stabbed, but not with a knife," Alex said.

"She was stabbed with a screwdriver," I added. "Which means Mary Riley might be a counterfeiter, but she did not kill Wanda Wegman."

Sheriff Kramer and Special Agent Vargas spent the next half hour going over the account of the murder with both Mary and Bubba. It was clear that neither of them knew the murder weapon was a flathead screwdriver. Mary didn't even know what a flathead screwdriver was, and had almost certainly never picked one up in her entire life.

When they had reached an impasse, the three of us met once again.

"Neither of them is Wanda's killer," Alex said.

Rebecca sighed. "What do you want to do now?"

Alex pulled out his wallet. "We get something to eat. The Hopeless Sheriff Department is paying. Hope, you think you could grab something from Bess and bring it over?"

"Sure."

Rebecca flashed a smile. "Mind if I join you, Hope?"

"Perfect. You can help me carry back all the grease."

As the two of us walked to the Library, I gave Rebecca the quick and dirty history of how Granny and Bess came to run a bar. I realized I was talking a lot, and I realized why. There was something I wanted to ask her… and, at the same time, *didn't* want to ask her.

But after we'd ordered cheeseburgers and fries from Bess, and had taken seats at the bar to wait for our food, I hesitantly steered the conversation toward the uncomfortable subject of her and Alex.

"So…" I said. "How long did you and Alex work together?"

"Well, we didn't work *together* that much, but we worked in the same office for three years."

"And why'd you make the switch to the Secret Service?"

"Are you kidding me? It's the Secret Service."

"Yeah, that does sound cooler than state police."

"So what's your story?" Rebecca asked. "After I talked to you on the phone I googled you. I saw you've written for the *Portland News Gazette*… and yet here you are in Hopeless, Idaho."

I chuckled. "I'm not really sure *how* that happened. But what it boils down to is, maybe I was a little too good at my job."

"How so?"

"I did a story on the Medola crime family… that hit a little too close to home. They didn't want it to go to print. I was fired, and the story didn't run."

"The Medolas are a nasty bunch."

"You know them?"

"They come on our radar for fraud. Haven't been able to get anything to stick."

We sipped on our Diet Cokes for a little while longer. I hadn't gotten anywhere in learning if there was a history between her and Alex. Maybe that was for the best.

But to my surprise, it was Rebecca who brought him up.

"If you don't mind me asking… I saw the way you were looking at Alex. Is there something going on between the two of you?"

I shook my head. "In all honesty? I have no idea."

"How could you not know?"

I laughed. "Because I'm the world's dumbest female when it comes to these things. I thought maybe there was something going on, but…"

"But now?"

I shrugged. "Now, I think murder investigations are easier to figure out than men."

She laughed. "Truer words…"

Bess brought us a paper bag full of burgers and fries, then leaned over and kissed me on the forehead. Rebecca and I left the bar and started walking back.

But then Rebecca stopped. "Did um… I take it Alex told you about us?"

And there it was. There was an "us."

I tried to act casual. "About?"

"The two of us. We dated. Pretty seriously. Heck, I thought we might even end up getting married. Then the opportunity opened up for me at the Secret Service and… and I don't know what happened."

I didn't know what to say. "And you're telling me this why?"

"Because I know Alex, okay?" She let out a breath. "I know him really, really well. And I saw the way he was looking at me tonight. Between us girls, I just don't think he's over me. And… and I think the two of us deserve another chance."

She grabbed the bag out of my hand. "I guess what I'm saying is… I think Alex and I can handle it from here."

~◦ CHAPTER THIRTY ◦~

Katie answered her phone after two rings. "Heard you guys made a big arrest. It's all anybody here at the pumpkin patch is talking about!"

"Why are you at the pumpkin patch on a Friday night?"

"Because my idiot husband invited a couple of guys over to our house to help him set up his beer-making equipment."

"Wait, what? Chris is going to start brewing his own beer?"

"Hope, don't get me wrong. I love my husband. And I really love beer. I just don't love the idea of my husband *making* beer. I explained to him that I could go down to the gas station and get a case of Coors Light for under thirty bucks. Or, he could spend a *thousand* bucks and spend a month making a liter of crappy beer."

"Coors Light *is* crappy beer."

"That was kind of my point."

"I assume that went over well."

"He whined about needing something to do other than

work and children, work and children."

"And I assume *that* went over well."

"I threw a shoe at his head. And then, demonstrating how mature I've become, I decided *not* to throw a second shoe at his head. Instead, I brought my children to Bubba's for some apple donuts."

"That's a lot of money for donuts."

"Mary gave me some all-day passes the other day. I think they're officially called 'We're sorry your five-year-old found a dead body in our pumpkin patch' passes. Anyway, I'm just glad I got them before you nailed her for murder. I can't believe little old Mary killed someone."

"I don't think she did," I said.

"Really? Is that why you're calling?"

"No, I'm calling because of stupid Alex."

"What did he do now?"

"Buy me some apple donuts and I'll tell you."

"You're coming to Bubba's?"

"I'm a single woman and it's Friday night. What else could I possibly have to do?"

I met up with Katie outside the haunted mine. She had a stroller full of donuts in front of her, leaving no room for baby Celia, who was in her mama's arms instead.

"A donut stroller?" I said.

"Gotta keep precious cargo somewhere. Here, Celia needs some Aunt Hope time." Without asking, she handed the big smiling blob of fat rolls and chubby cheeks to me.

Celia smiled at once.

Katie handed me a donut. "She likes you."

I kissed Celia's big fat cheek and gave her a hug. If I was being honest, I liked her too. I liked all of Katie's kids, despite them being little animals at times. And I sort of missed being around them this week. But I wasn't about to tell Katie that.

Katie raised an eyebrow. "So… stupid Alex?"

I nodded. "Stupid Alex."

Katie laughed. "You know, I remember someone else you used to call stupid." She smiled. "Jimmy."

"Don't even."

"I'm just saying. What did stupid Alex do this time?"

First I told her about the question I'd asked Alex while having chocolate cake on her couch—the one about whether or not he'd ever been in a serious relationship. I told her how he dodged the question at first, then finally told me when I pressed him the next day.

"That explains the two wine glasses," she said. "I figured you were just double-fisting it that night."

Then I told her about Special Agent Rebecca Vargas.

"Geez, Hope. How does something like that even happen? You randomly call the Secret Service, and you get put through to… Alex's ex? And then you just happen to invite to Hopeless the one person in the world you *least* want to come to Hopeless?"

"Only I could be this lucky."

"Wow. And she really told you that Alex wasn't over her? Just like that?"

I nodded. "It was cold."

"No, it was evil. That's something Gemima would do."

"And she seemed so nice before that. You know, while we were just arresting people for murder and counterfeiting."

"So what are you going to do?"

"I guess what I usually do."

"Push down all semblance of authentic human emotions for the next twelve years until you're interested in another guy?"

"Harsh."

Katie grabbed another donut and took a bite. "But true. Hope, if Alex really is interested in this girl… then what can you do? Move on. And if he's *not* interested in this girl, it'll work itself out."

"That's a pretty balanced and mature view for a woman who threw a shoe at her husband's head tonight."

"Married women with three children are allowed some inconsistencies. You, my friend, are not. You are Hope Walker, you are single, you are beautiful, and you have a heart that's bigger than you could possibly know. And you deserve to love and be loved. So whatever you do, don't hide that heart. Don't act like it doesn't exist. And don't act like you don't deserve to be happy. I don't know if Alex Kramer and you are any good for each other, but I've seen the way he looks at you. I remember how Jimmy looked at you. And I know how my kids have talked about you this week."

Katie's eyes got a little wet, and that caused my throat to tighten. I closed my eyes and tried to control my breathing.

Then the screams of children brought me back to the moment. I opened my eyes to see Lucy and Dominic running out of the haunted mine.

"Aunt Hope!" they shouted.

I knelt down, and they both ran and gave me and Celia a big hug. I had to admit, it felt really, really good. Katie looked at us and wiped a tear from her cheek. I stood up and took a deep breath, then handed Celia back to her.

"So, Hope, what are you going to do?"

"Can we go to the haunted corn maze?" asked Lucy.

"Can we find another dead body?" asked Dominic.

I laughed. "Those sound like fun ideas for you guys. As for me... I know what I have to do."

Katie cocked an eyebrow. "Be a real human being with the full spectrum of emotions, tell Alex how you feel, and lay your heart on the line?"

I smiled. "I think you know me better than that."

"I was afraid of that."

"You see, Mrs. Rodgers, I'm an investigative reporter. And though Mary Riley was doing some crooked stuff—I mean, she was up to her eyeballs in counterfeit money—you were right about her."

"I was?"

"Mary Riley is not a murderer. Somebody else killed Wanda Wegman, and I'm going to find out who."

I said goodbye to Katie and the children. Dominic seemed especially upset that we wouldn't be looking for another dead body together. He gave me a long hug goodbye. He was an odd boy—equal parts dangerous and strange. But he was also special and sweet. In his own way.

I walked back down Apple Donut Lane to Lucinda's Famous Apple Donuts. Lucinda was working the front counter, and when she saw me coming, she had someone take her place and stepped out to meet me.

"How's everything going with Mary and Bubba?" she asked with concern.

"She's admitted to the whole counterfeit operation."

"Wow. It's… unreal. Everyone around here is in shock."

"And you?"

"Especially me. I never saw it coming."

"And you know this place pretty well?"

"I thought I did. Like I told you, I like to know a little bit about every part of this pumpkin patch."

"But you never suspected anything like this?"

"Never in a million years. I especially never would have thought her capable of killing poor Wanda."

"You haven't heard?" I said.

"Heard what?"

"Mary didn't kill Wanda."

Lucinda's expression changed. "What? I thought you said…"

"I was wrong. After interviewing Bubba and Mary… it's clear she didn't do it."

Lucinda leaned in. "How can you be sure?"

"I… can't really say."

"Then who *did* do it?"

"That's why I'm here. You know this place as well as anyone. I know I've asked you before, but I'm asking you again. If Mary didn't do it… then who do you think could have killed Wanda Wegman?"

Lucinda put her hand to her chest. Then she shook her head.

"I don't know. I really don't know."

I caught the last couple minutes of Johnny Driscoll's final show for the night. His mobile robot got into a laser tag fight with a robot alien space cowboy that I hadn't seen before. The kids went crazy and gave him a huge round of applause.

He rolled his eyes when he saw me coming.

I held up my palms in a sign of peace. "Relax."

"I thought your mission to destroy our pumpkin patch was done."

"What do you mean?"

"Well, you hauled off the owners. That won't be good for business."

"So it's okay to commit a crime, as long as you run a pumpkin patch?"

"There's no way Mary killed Wanda."

"And how can you be so sure?" I asked.

"Because I'm smarter than most people. Remember?"

"Well, Johnny, this time you're right."

"I am?"

"Mary admitted to counterfeiting. All of it. But she flatly denies killing Wanda."

"And you believe her?"

"I do."

"So… why are you talking to me? Hoping I'll confess to the crime?"

"That would sure make my job easier."

"Well, sorry to disappoint you, but I didn't kill Wanda and I think you know that. If Kip and her really were dating, and if she really broke up with him, then I'd start there. Now, if you don't mind, I've got a lot to do before I get out of here."

"Big plans tonight?"

"Do I look like the kind of guy who has big plans?"

I found Kip Granger unloading the last tractor full of hayrack riders. He was wearing the same blue overalls, white shirt, and green John Deere cap that he always wore. I wondered how many hayrack rides he had given in his life. Probably thousands. And I wondered if I had overthought this from the beginning. I remembered Earl Denton's maxim. Occam's razor. The simplest explanation is usually correct.

Wanda's body was found in the pumpkin patch. And nobody spent more time in the pumpkin patch than Kip Granger, the farmer.

One of the strongest motives in the world was love gone wrong. Kip liked Wanda. Maybe loved her. She broke it off. His heart was broken.

Occam's razor.

I waited until everybody departed the hayrack and Kip climbed down from his tractor.

"Didn't expect to see you again so soon," he said as he took out a handkerchief and blew his nose.

"We've got a problem," I said.

"What kind of problem?"

"Mary Riley didn't kill Wanda."

"I thought you said…"

"I know what I said… but I was wrong. Mary admitted to the counterfeiting, but she didn't murder Wanda."

"You sure about that?"

"Pretty sure, yeah."

Kip pulled out his pocket knife and started to dig out the dirt from under his fingernails again. Then I noticed how suddenly alone we were. The hayrack ride area was empty.

"You seem frustrated," I said.

"Aren't you? I thought you figured it out. I thought you solved it."

"I solved part of it—but not the most important part. And I'm here to ask for your help. Is there anything else you can tell me, anything at all, that might help lead me to the real killer?"

"I'm just an old farmer. I've already told you everything I know."

"I believe you, Kip. I'm just… at a dead end. I don't know what to do next."

"Hmm."

"Hmm what?"

He folded up his pocket knife and returned it to his

overalls. "Listen, I don't know anything about solving crimes. But I'm pretty good at fixing things. There's so much equipment in farming that you pretty much *have* to know how to fix things. Anyway, sometimes I take a machine apart to fix it, and I'm sure I've done it right. Then I put it back together, turn it on, and realize I didn't really solve the problem. I fixed something, but I didn't fix it completely."

"And what do you do then?"

"There's only one thing I can do. I have to retrace all my steps. Along the way, I always spot something. Something I forgot to do. Something I broke. Or something I overlooked the first time."

"Do you think you could help me figure out what I overlooked?"

"Like I said, I'm just an old farmer, but..." He smiled. "Let's retrace your steps."

~⊙ CHAPTER THIRTY-ONE ⊙~

Kip and I sat on a couple of hay bales while I walked him through my investigation from start to finish. Finding the body. Talking to Bubba and Mary. Finding out it was Wanda. Learning she was stabbed. Interviewing person after person after person. Getting both Mary and Bubba to confess.

I didn't tell him *why* I was certain that Mary and Bubba didn't do it. That would mean revealing that little detail about the real murder weapon, and I needed to hold that one back. Just in case.

I even told Kip about the high-stakes poker game. Yes, I'd promised Flo I wouldn't say anything, but forget the first rule of Poker Night, I was desperate, this was a murder investigation, and Kip didn't really seem the gossiping kind. I told him about getting the fake twenty from Flo, hearing her story about Wanda, searching Wanda's cottage for any evidence of counterfeiting, and finding none. I told him about checking her computer and finding searches for mechanical engineering and recipes and baking and welding and pumpkin patches… *and* counterfeiting.

"Which makes sense," I said. "If she had just discovered Mary had paid her with fake money, she wanted to learn as much as she could before she confronted her."

"Yeah, that makes sense, all right." Then Kip scratched at his chin. "What were the other searches about again?"

"Mechanical stuff, mostly. Hydraulics and… I don't even know."

He shook his head. "No, there was something about recipes."

"Yeah, lots of stuff about recipes and baking. Those were mostly more recent. Guess she was getting into cooking."

He rubbed his forehead with his thumb and forefinger. "That doesn't make sense. Wanda wouldn't have been looking at anything related to cooking."

"Why not?"

"Because Wanda *hated* cooking. I don't just mean she couldn't cook, which I'm sure was true, I mean she refused to. She wouldn't even touch a microwave. She liked to eat food plenty well, just didn't want to have anything to do with making it."

"I don't know, Kip. When I start wasting time on the internet, I search for all kinds of things."

"Did she look at recipes just one time?" he asked.

"Well, no. There were lots of searches over several weeks."

"That doesn't sound random to me. And I knew Wanda pretty well. I just don't see her wasting time looking at recipes. That doesn't fit."

"Okay, but… I mean, they're recipes. What does that have to do with anything?"

Kip shrugged. "I have no idea. I'm just a farmer. You want to know something about cooking, you best talk to Lucinda."

I checked the time on my phone. Five minutes to nine. Closing time. "I'll never make it back to Apple Donut Lane before everything closes."

Kip smiled. "Then you're in luck. Lucinda's not at the donut shop this time of night. When she can, she likes to take the last shift of the night over there."

He pointed over my shoulder.

"At the corn maze."

As I hustled over to the corn maze, I called Darwin.

"Hope," he said, "I don't have much time. I've got a hot date."

"Seriously?"

"No, it's just you're always teasing me. I thought I'd try to get you back."

"And you did, Darwin. Big time. I'm actually running short on time too. Remember that search history you pulled up on Wanda Wegman's computer? Can you pull that up again for me right now?"

"Sure. Just log in and give me access like you did before."

"I'm not at her computer right now."

"I can't turn on her computer remotely, Hope."

"Darn it! I thought you'd be able to help."

"Oh, I didn't say I couldn't help. As it turns out, I had a

feeling you weren't done with this yet, so when you logged me in last time, I copied a bunch of stuff over. Including her entire search history."

"Darwin, you are the best boyfriend ever."

"Stop that right now. What do you need to know?"

"There were some searches for recipes and baking stuff. I didn't look at them carefully. Could you skim through them and give me an idea what they were about?"

"Um, let's see…" He paused. "Uh… mostly it's stuff about donuts. Recipes for donuts."

"What kind of donuts?"

"Looks like apple donuts."

"You're sure?"

"It's right in front of me, and believe it or not I am capable of reading words, so yeah… I'm pretty sure."

"Anything else about baking or recipes or donuts?"

"Um, well…" Another pause. "Okay, here's one for a pumpkin patch near Omaha. The landing page is for Annie's Apple Donuts."

"Annie's Apple Donuts?"

"Yep. And here's a search for an award called Best Donut in America."

"Is that from 2014?"

"As a matter of fact, it is."

"And who was the winner that year?"

"Somebody called Lucinda Meadows. Does that mean anything to you?"

"It means a lot to me. You see anything else that might be related?"

"Um, no, pretty much just more of the same. Recipes and… okay, this one's a little different. This site is for a food testing lab."

"A food testing lab?"

"That is what the words say, Hope. She went to a site for someplace called Northwest Food Testing Labs. It looks like you can send in food and they can break down the ingredients, give you nutritional info, that kind of thing. Is that helpful?"

"Very, very helpful. Hey, when you copied her stuff over, did you grab her email?"

"Of course. That was the first thing I did."

"And did you look through it?"

"Yeah… um, no. I sort of forgot."

I sighed. "Listen, I've got to go talk to someone real quick before they leave. Could you quickly search her email for anything related to food or recipes or apple donuts or this food testing lab?"

"When did do you need this done by?"

"Thirty seconds ago."

I found Lucinda just as she was about to turn off the lights to the corn maze.

"Hi, Hope! Burning the midnight oil." She nodded with her head toward the hayracks. "Talking to Kip?"

"Yeah, he was just trying to help me sort through things."

"And did it help?"

"Honestly, I think I'm more confused than ever."

"I don't know how you do it."

"Do what?"

"Investigate murders and crimes and mysteries all the time. What I do, making food, is much more straightforward. You have a recipe, you follow the directions, and if you do everything right, you get the result you wanted. But you? You can work your tail off and *still* never know if you'll come up with an answer."

"Funny you should mention recipes and food. That's part of what has me confused."

"How so?"

"I'm trying to figure out why Wanda was so interested in baking and recipes at the end of her life."

"What makes you think she was?"

"Her internet search history. Last few weeks of her life, she became suddenly interested in donuts."

"Donuts?"

"Apple donuts, to be more precise. And since you're the donut queen, I thought I'd ask you why."

Lucinda shrugged. "Wanda was pretty handy. Maybe she wanted to make donuts."

"But apple donuts? You already make apple donuts. America's Best Donut in 2014 if I'm not mistaken. Why learn to make donuts when you've already got the best donut in America just down Apple Donut Lane?"

She shrugged again. "I can't say. Maybe Wanda liked to tinker in the kitchen."

"But that's just the thing. She didn't tinker in the kitchen. She didn't do *anything* in the kitchen. I would have thought you knew that."

She looked puzzled. "I don't know what to tell you. What does this have to do with your investigation?"

I had a feeling I knew *exactly* what this had to do with my investigation. Wanda's search history had included two new topics in the last weeks of her life: apple donut recipes and counterfeit money. She'd confronted someone about the counterfeiting. I *thought* that had gotten her killed.

Had she also confronted someone about apple donut recipes?

"She also looked up a donut shop in a pumpkin patch outside of Omaha, Nebraska," I said. "Annie's Apple Donuts. Do you know that place?"

Lucinda frowned and nodded, as if thinking. "Yeah... I think I have. You know, Bubba and Wanda have visited a lot of pumpkin patches through the years. They've probably been there."

"That's interesting. I'll talk to them about it." I paused, then added, "Oh, and there's one more thing that's the hardest to figure of all."

"What's that?"

"You ever heard of a place called Northwest Food Testing Labs?"

Her face twitched. No eye contact. "Doesn't ring a bell."

"They test food and figure out what the food's made of. What ingredients are in it. Wanda was looking at their web site shortly before she died."

"Huh. That's weird." She looked about on the ground, like a woman who was lost.

"Yeah," I agreed. "That's really weird."

My phone buzzed. Darwin. I raised my finger to Lucinda. "Just a second."

I turned and whispered to Darwin. "Find anything?"

"Plenty. But I suspect the one you're going to be interested in is an email from Wanda to someone from Northwest Food Testing."

"Tell me."

"Apparently Wanda sent them two apple donuts, and asked them to compare the two. The lab tested them, and shared its results. The donuts are identical. Exact same ingredients in the exact same proportion. According to the lab, a perfect match."

Boom. There it was. The kind of puzzle piece that makes all the rest of the pieces suddenly fall into place.

"That's exactly what I needed, Darwin. Call me back if you find anything more."

I ended the call and turned back around.

Lucinda was standing right in front of me, holding a pitchfork a foot away from my face.

"Put the phone down, Hope. Put it down *now*."

⌒ CHAPTER THIRTY-TWO ⌒

Lucinda backed me up into the corn maze, the sharp tines of the pitchfork never far from my chest. Thankfully, the overhead lights were still on. But still, it was a corn maze.

Worse, it was *the* corn maze.

"Why'd you have to keep asking questions?" Lucinda said. Her eyes were fierce, her face hard and mean. No joy. No happiness. Nothing friendly whatsoever. The Donut Queen was gone, and in her place was someone else entirely.

"I had to find out the truth," I said. "That's my job."

"A grumpy old woman was dead. Dead for three years. You didn't see anyone carrying on about it, begging to know the truth."

"Because they thought she'd run off."

"I don't see that it matters. Gone is gone."

"You murdered her!"

"I took care of a problem, Hope. Nothing more, nothing less. That's what I do."

"I thought you were supposed to be the Donut Queen. A woman who makes a day at the pumpkin patch just a little bit better."

"I am that. But you can't have sunshine without a little darkness."

This woman was cold, calculating, and, as I now feared... more than a little crazy. I should never have confronted her alone. That's what Wanda did, and we all know how that turned out. I should have gotten Alex first. Or at least brought Kip.

I couldn't just let her take charge. She would back me into the maze, get me out of sight of everyone, and then...

And then she would kill me. Like she killed Wanda.

I had to make my move.

I looked over her shoulder and widened my eyes as if I'd seen someone. She wasn't fooled, but she did hesitate just long enough for me to spin around and take off—straight into the maze.

Of course, I wasn't worried about following the twists and turns. I busted right through the rows of corn. I needed to put as much distance between her and I as I possibly could.

And then, with a loud click... everything went dark.

Lucinda had shut off the overhead lights shut, and the corn maze was shrouded in inky blackness.

In my youth, the horrible corn maze was haunted by fog—but at least I could still see. This was far worse. There must have been heavy cloud cover, because I saw no moon, no stars, no light.

And in the distance, Lucinda's footsteps crunched against the dirt.

"Running won't get you very far, Hope. I designed the

corn maze this year. I know it backward and forward. I can do it in the dark. You can't."

My heart pounded away in my chest, and my breath was rapid and shallow. I spun around, trying to get my bearings. I stretched out my arms—and felt the tentacles of a monster. In my mind, I knew it was just corn. But my imagination was telling me something very different.

I turned until I felt open space before me, then slowly made my way forward.

But I had no idea where I was going.

"I hope you're not too scared, Hope. Remember, all of us die. It can't be that bad, right? When I watched Wanda die, it honestly didn't seem so bad. She hurt for a little bit, and then it was over. Easy-peasy. Heck, lots of things in life hurt for a long, long time. Don't worry—I won't let you suffer. I'll make sure you won't hurt for long either."

I sprinted forward, crashed face-first into the corn, and screamed.

Lucinda laughed. "Well, now I know exactly where you are. Now be a good girl and let me finish this."

It was clear that I couldn't escape her in this maze. I had no idea where I was or where I was going. I had to do something else. I had to get her talking.

And at least I might have a chance.

"So the testing lab," I said. My voice shook. "Wanda told you about it?"

"Can you believe the nerve of that nosy old hag? Testing my donuts behind my back?"

"She tested your donut against one from Annie's Apple

Donuts, didn't she? The place in Omaha? And the lab told her they were identical."

"Mine are better."

"If they're identical, how could yours be better?"

Lucinda laughed. "Simple. Because mine are made with love."

"You're a psychopath, Lucinda. Your donuts were never made with love. In fact they're the most calculated donuts in history. Because you stole the recipe. Didn't you?"

"It's only stealing if you get caught. And even then it's not stealing if the person who catches you gets a screwdriver stuck in the belly ... or something like that." She laughed. "I forget the saying exactly."

"You must have been on one of those trips years ago to visit other pumpkin patches. Bubba said it was a great way to learn. You ate some apple donuts in Omaha."

"They were the best donuts I'd ever had," said Lucinda. Her footsteps crunched relentlessly toward me.

"And you didn't forget about them," I said. "How could you? They're delicious. And then one day, you got the idea to compete in the Best Donut of America competition. So you stole Annie's recipe."

"Well, not so fast, Hope. I tried my own recipe. Many versions of it. But I never could recapture the taste of Annie's donut. And why would I settle for second best? So I found a woman who worked at Annie's, and she was willing to part with the exact recipe for a few hundred dollars. It was really quite easy."

"And then you submitted the donuts to the contest,

claiming the recipe as your own."

"Well, it *is* my own now, isn't it? I bought it, didn't I? It's amazing how easy it is to cheat."

"That's it. Wanda hated cheaters. I bet she visited that same pumpkin patch in Omaha. Ate those same apple donuts. The woman couldn't cook, but she liked food. I'm guessing she noticed right away that your donuts were awfully similar to Annie's donuts. Maybe even the same. But she probably thought that was coincidence. She would never have suspected such devious behavior from someone she had worked with for years. Until... until she discovered that maybe she should have suspected *exactly* that. Because one of her co-workers was a counterfeiter.

"That's what happened. She got caught with fake bills. Bills that came from her employer. That made her furious. She hated cheaters. And she was no longer willing to give anyone the benefit of the doubt. So she went home and she did some digging. Not just into Mary Riley the counterfeiter, but into someone else. Lucinda Meadows the recipe-stealer. And she caught you both. Dead to rights.

"She confronted Mary. Told her to stop counterfeiting immediately. And Mary agreed. But when Wanda confronted you, the meeting had a very different outcome."

Suddenly, Lucinda emerged from the darkness before me. I couldn't see much, but I make out her shape, the pitchfork that was aimed at my heart, and the whites of her teeth as she smiled.

"I'm surprised Mary had the guts for a counterfeit scheme," she said. "I've gained respect for her. I always thought of her as a bit of a pushover. I, however, am not a pushover. I wasn't about to let old Wanda Wegman threaten *me*. Yes, she confronted me. I couldn't believe she'd put it all together. But I also knew what I had to do. I didn't panic. Didn't sob like some fool. I had a problem, so I *fixed the problem*.

"I'd been fixing some kitchen equipment and had a screwdriver nearby. I grabbed it, stabbed her, and dragged her body over to the train. I loaded her on the train, drove her over to the pumpkin patch, and buried her body. If I made a mistake, it was only that I didn't bury it deep enough. Now..." Her teeth glinted in the darkness once more. "I'm sorry, Hope, but that is the end of our little story. And this is the end of the road for you. For what it's worth, I respect you. Hell, I respected Wanda. But you're a problem. And problems need to be fixed."

The overhead lights flicked on and voices screamed, "Aunt Hope! Aunt Hope!"

I didn't hesitate. Batting the pitchfork to one side, I threw myself at Lucinda, pinning her arms to her sides. She stumbled backward but didn't fall. She was strong. She freed one of her hands and punched me in the head, knocking me onto my butt in the dirt. She raised the pitchfork above me.

But I was quick. I jammed my heel as hard as I could into her knee. She howled and buckled over.

The kids' screaming was getting closer.

I scrambled to my feet just as Lucinda raised the pitchfork again. She swung it at me, and I ducked under the tines and grabbed the handle. We were face to face, both of us trying to gain control of that pitchfork. I needed to get it away from her.

And then she headbutted me right in the nose.

I felt to the ground, my head spinning.

Lucinda raised the pitchfork once more.

I saw Lucy and Dominic crashing through the corn on my right. Lucinda saw them too. What she didn't see was the person flying in from my left.

Katie.

My best friend came sprinting through the corn, clenched fist raised high, and before Lucinda had time to react, Katie crushed Lucinda's jaw with the greatest punch I've ever seen.

Lucinda crumpled to the dirt like a rag doll.

I rose groggily to my feet.

Katie was standing over Lucinda like Cassius Clay standing over Sonny Liston. "You think I should sit on her just to make sure?"

Lucinda's eyes were rolled into the back of her head. She was breathing, but it was shallow.

"I don't think she's going anywhere," I said. I hugged my best friend from behind. "Katie, that was probably the single greatest thing I have ever seen in my life."

"Better than when you punched out Gemima?"

"Way better."

"Thank God, because Hope, I'm pretty sure I just broke every bone in my hand."

~ CHAPTER THIRTY-THREE ~

So how exactly did Katie come to deliver the punch heard round the world? As we stood safely outside the corn maze, Katie explained that when she and her kids left Bubba's and got in the car, Dominic started to shake.

He was scared.

"Now, remember," Katie said, "this is the boy who thinks the first twenty minutes of *Saving Private Ryan* are tremendous fun."

"You haven't actually let him watch *Saving Private Ryan*... have you?"

Katie snapped her fingers. "You're getting off topic. Focus on the story. So, my weird kid doesn't just get scared for any old reason. I ask him what's wrong, and he said he's got a funny feeling. I ask him about what. And he says he's got a funny feeling about Aunt Hope."

"He said that?"

"He did. At first I thought, what are the chances... but then he started throwing a crazytown tantrum... so I turned the car around, and we drove back to Bubba's. The lady up front wouldn't let us back in—'no ifs, ands, or buts'—so I told her she could kiss my big white davenport and call the sheriff if she had to. And when she started to call the sheriff, the kids and I ran on in.

"I saw Kip Granger, and I told him I was looking for you, that we had a bad feeling. He said you'd gone to see Lucinda at the corn maze. And Dominic just started running faster than I've ever seen before. Lucy and I chased after and could barely keep up."

"Wait. Where was Celia during all this?"

"Oh. I gave her to Kip Granger." She turned and pointed. Kip was standing off to one side, snuggling the baby. Celia looked as happy as I'd ever seen her. So did Kip.

"What if he was the deranged killer?" I said.

"Then I would have just made a very big mistake, wouldn't I? So let's instead focus on the bright side."

Just at that moment, Sheriff Kramer emerged from the corn maze, escorting a woozy-looking Lucinda. Her hands were cuffed behind her back, and the right side of her face looked like a car had run over it.

Alex acknowledged me with a tip of his head. But that was all. He had work to do.

And when that work was done? Who knows?

I was confused. I think Alex was too.

Katie continued. "So we get down to the corn maze and all the lights are off. But I see the faint reflection of a phone on the ground. Your phone. Then I heard voices from inside the corn maze. I flip those lights on, and me and the kids go crazy. I figure, whatever's going on in there cannot be good."

"And then?"

"Hope, the rest is a blur. The kids took off through the corn maze screaming their brains out, and I just started running straight through corn like Bugs Bunny running through walls. I heard the sound of a struggle, and… what can I say? Dominic's funny feeling became *my* funny feeling."

"And then you punched Lucinda like Ivan Drago in *Rocky IV*."

Katie did her best Drago impression. "I must break you."

"Katie Rodgers, I'm really sorry your hand is going to hurt for a while. Because *you* are my hero."

"Not just me." Katie nodded down to her two older children, who were waiting patiently for once in their lives. I told Lucy how brave she was and I gave her a hug. But I saved my biggest hug for Dominic. My five-year-old hero.

"You saved me, Dominic. You really saved me."

He blushed. Then he reached up to Katie and pulled on her shirt. "Can we have a story tonight? Please?"

"Do you want Aunt Hope to tell the story about Godzilla Versus Dominic's Old Dead Arm?"

Dominic smiled. "No, we want to hear the new story: 'When Mama Hit the Bad Woman Really, Really Hard.'"

Things moved fast the next day.

Sheriff Kramer officially arrested Lucinda Meadows for the murder of Wanda Wegman and the attempted murder of me.

Special Agent Vargas worked out a plea deal for Mary Riley. If she could deliver Derby Sledge, the federal prosecutor would agree to no jail time. But she would have to pay a steep fine, and she would be assigned enough community service to keep her busy for a very long time.

Dr. Bridges made a house call to Katie, put her hand in a splint, and gave her a prescription for happy drugs. Chris temporarily paused his beer-making enterprise in order to wait on Katie hand and foot.

As well he should. Katie Rodgers was a hero.

She was my hero.

I spent most of the day Saturday writing up two stories for the *Hopeless Gazette*. And when Earl had read them both, all he could say was…

"Holy smokes!"

"That's good, Earl?"

"That's very good, Hope. We'll run the pumpkin patch story now."

"And the goat story?"

"We wait. But this is a very good start."

I left the newspaper offices just in time to see Special Agent Vargas give Alex a big hug. Then she got in her car and drove away.

Alex saw me and jogged right over. "I'm glad you're okay," he said.

"No thanks to me. I have a habit of getting myself into stupid situations."

"I might have phrased it that way myself a month ago."

"But now?"

"I think you have a habit of getting yourself *out of* stupid situations."

"Not this time. This time it was Katie and her kids. If not for them, I don't want to think about—"

He cut me off. "I don't either."

"So, you and Rebecca?"

"Yeah, she mentioned she said something to you. She shouldn't have done that."

"You should have told me."

"I was trying to."

"But you didn't. You didn't tell me that you had a serious relationship just before coming to Hopeless. You didn't stand up for me in front of Gemima and the whole town."

"That's not fair."

"Maybe. But it is what it is."

"So that's it?"

"Alex, I'm hungry… and I need to eat."

"You want to get a bite?"

I looked down at my phone. At the text from Mark Pendergast. It was Saturday. He was in town. And he wanted to have dinner.

I looked back up at Alex. "Unfortunately, I already have plans."

I drove three short blocks to Mazzarelli's Italian Restaurant. Mark Pendergast was seated at a booth against the wall. He was wearing jeans and a dark blazer, and his hair was slightly slicked back. He looked good. I couldn't tell if this was a date or a job interview, but at the moment, I was ready for both.

I told him about my two stories. He loved them, and asked if Earl would let his show run with either of them. I said I didn't know. Maybe. If the price was right.

Regardless, he said if this was the kind of work I did, he really wanted to give me a shot.

"On TV?" I said.

"Yes, on TV. In New York. Come out soon, give us a screen test… and if the network loves you as much as I do, then we move forward."

My dream was coming true. My purgatory in Hopeless was coming to an end. In its place was the big city. Big job. Big money. Everything I had ever dreamed of.

And yet, at the moment, all I could think about was a little boy who'd had a funny feeling, a best friend who'd thrown a mighty punch, and a man with green eyes that I just couldn't shake.

My phone buzzed. The caller ID said it was Nick the barista. Why was he calling me?

I looked at Mark. "Do you mind if I…?"

He smiled and waved me away. "I get it, the work never ends. Better answer that."

I stood up and answered. "Nick?"

"I was told to call you to give you a message."

"What are you talking about?"

"That hot chick. She gave me ten bucks to call you and give a message."

I walked to the window and looked up the street at A Hopeless Cup. It was closed.

"Nobody's at the coffee shop, Nick."

"Yeah, I know. The hot chick came in earlier, but she told me to call you with the message tonight."

I continued staring at the dark empty shadows inside A Hopeless Cup. "What's the message?"

"It's weird."

"Okay. But what is it?"

"She wrote it down so I wouldn't forget it. Not that I would have. It's only two words."

"Nick… just tell me the message already."

He did—and I almost dropped the phone.

The message was, in fact, only two words. Two simple but creepy words.

Bang Bang.

THE END

Dear Reader:
A Note From Daniel Carson

Thank you for reading *A Hopeless Discovery*, the third book in the *Hope Walker Mysteries*. The fourth Hope Walker Mystery, *A Hopeless Game*, will be released in October of 2019. If you sign up for my newsletter, I will send you an update when the fourth book is available.

Daniel Carson Newsletter Link:
http://eepurl.com/dtZWfH

The last year has been crazy for my family. We experienced a small house fire in early November. Our little family of ten lived with the in-laws for a few days, a hotel for a month, and a rental house for three months while I worked hard on getting everything ready to move our family back in. We got back into our house (Yay!) and we feel so blessed that the fire wasn't worse and that nobody was hurt. Smoke alarms are a glorious thing and firefighters are great at what they do. Again, my wife and I feel very fortunate and quite blessed.

But once we got into our house this spring, life seemed like it was going a hundred miles an hour every day. I'm sure you all know the drill. School, practices, games, work, sick kids, school cancellations, basically, life! But for some reason, the pace of life seems to accelerate ever more quickly for our family with each passing year.

One contributing factor, our oldest daughter graduated from High School this spring. And, with the oldest one graduating…and the youngest one entering kindergarten, times are changing around our house.

And amidst all of this, I didn't get the third Hope Walker book to you as quickly as I thought I would. You'll see that's a recurring theme from me. Sorry! I've once again readjusted my publishing schedule to better reflect the realities of my life. And I think I have a handle on it now. Fingers crossed! At this point, expect Hope Walker 4 in October 2019 and expect Hope Walker 5 in December of 2019. Book 5 will conclude the first season of the Hope Walker Mysteries and I'm really excited for how this first season is going to wrap up. I hope you enjoy reading about Hope, and Katie, and Granny as much as I enjoy writing about them!

Remember to sign up for my newsletter if you want updates or you can always come over to my Facebook Author page and say hello. I would love to hear from you.

Daniel Carson Facebook Author Page:
https://www.facebook.com/AuthorDanielCarson/

And remember that *Hope Walker Four: A Hopeless Game* comes out in October.

Thank you so much for reading!

Daniel

P.S. Reviews are awesome. More awesome than you can possibly understand. If you could leave a short review on Amazon, I would be thrilled. If you could leave a review on a billboard in Times Square, I would be overjoyed.

Made in United States
Troutdale, OR
04/21/2024

19349034R00174